Ain't No Savage Like The One I Got

Tina J

Copyright 2019

Warning:

This book is strictly Urban Fiction and the story is **NOT**

REAL!

Characters will not behave the way you want them to; nor will

they react to situations the way you think they should. Some of

them may be drug addicts, kingpins, savages, thugs, rich, poor,

ho's, sluts, haters, bitter ex-girlfriends or boyfriends, people

from the past and the list can go on and on. That is what Urban

Fiction mostly consists of. If this isn't anything you foresee

yourself interested in, then do yourself a favor and don't read it

because it's only going to piss you off. □□

Also, the book will not end the way you want so please be

advised that the outcome will be based solely on my own

thoughts and ideas. I hope you enjoy this book that y'all made

me write. Thanks so much to my readers, supporters, publisher

and fellow authors and authoress for the support. □□

Author Tina J

3

More books from me:

The Thug I Chose 1, 2 & 3

A Thin Line Between Me and My Thug 1 & 2

I Got Luv For My Shawty 1 & 2

Kharis and Caleb: A Different Kind of Love 1 & 2

Loving You Is A Battle 1 & 2 & 3

Violet and The Connect 1 & 2 & 3

You Complete Me

Love Will Lead You Back

This Thing Called Love

Are We In This Together 1,2 &3

Shawty Down To Ride For a Boss 1, 2 &3

When A Boss Falls in Love 1, 2 & 3

Let Me Be The One 1 & 2

We Got That Forever Love

Aint No Savage Like The One I Got 1&2

A Queen and A Hustla 1, 2 & 3

Thirsty For A Bad Boy 1&2

Hassan and Serena: An Unforgettable Love 1&2

Caught Up Loving A Beast 1, 2 & 3

A Street King And His Shawty 1 & 2

I Fell For The Wrong Bad Boy 1&2

I Wanna Love You 1 & 2

Addicted to Loving a Boss 1, 2, & 3

I Need That Gangsta Love 1&2

Creepin With The Plug 1 & 2

All Eyes On The Crown 1,2&3

When She's Bad, I'm Badder: Jiao and Dreek, A Crazy

Love Story 1,2&3

Still Luvin A Beast 1&2

Her Man, His Savage 1 & 2

Marco & Rakia: Not Your Ordinary, Hood Kinda Love 1,2

& 3

Feenin For A Real One 1, 2 & 3

A Kingpin's Dynasty 1, 2 & 3

What Kinda Love Is This: Captivating A Boss 1, 2 & 3

Frankie & Lexi: Luvin A Young Beast 1, 2 & 3

A Dope Boys Seduction 1, 2 & 3

My Brother's Keeper 1. 2 & 3

C'Yani & Meek: A Dangerous Hood Love 1, 2 & 3

When A Savage Falls for A Good Girl 1, 2 & 3

Eva & Deray 1 & 2

Blame It On His Gangsta Luv 1 & 2

Falling For The Wrong Hustla 1, 2 & 3

I Gave My Heart To A Jersey Killa 1, 2 & 3

Wolf

Ten years ago

"Rosco you have to pay them the money. If not, they're going to kill me and the kids." I heard my mom begging my father.

I wasn't sure what was going on but at twelve years old I was smart enough to know my dad owed someone money. I stood at the door while my ten-year-old brother and fourteen-year-old sister sat on the bed with pure fear in their eyes. One would think because my sister was the oldest, she would be telling us what to do. Instead she held my brother close to her as he cried.

"Roberta get the fuck out of here. I'm not paying anybody shit. I gave him the money but because it was a day late that motherfucker is trying to add a five thousand dollars late fee and I only owed him a thousand. Who the fuck charges interest like that?"

I was a math genius in school so when my dad put it

out there that someone tried charging him four times the amount he owed, I agreed with him not paying. Unfortunately, it came at the expense of us and we already knew he wasn't going to pay. I didn't think he had the money either, but he wasn't going to tell my mom that.

Shit, my mom had section 8 and we lived in a two-family house where the landlord stayed on one side and we stayed on the other. However, it was still in the hood; just across the street from the projects.

My dad has been in the drug game damn near all my life and was still nickel and diming it. I mean who sells all these years and have nothing to show for it? My mom was getting about six hundred dollars in food stamps a month for us and working at McDonald's just to have some sort of income to continue receiving assistance.

Our house wasn't all that, but we had our own rooms, a bed, water to wash our ass, food to eat and my mom always made sure the lights were on. The people from social services had her sign up to get help with gas and electric and they had her on a budget, so we never worried about those getting cut off. Our clothes were not name brand at all, but my mom made sure we looked presentable. Our clothes were ironed, and our shoes may not have been Jordan's, but we did occasionally get Adidas or Pumas if they were on sale. We took very good care of our things just in case she fell on hard times it wouldn't show.

My father only gave her money for the holidays and our birthdays where she would splurge on us. I wasn't really sure what he did with the money he made, and I didn't care. I just know when I get older my siblings won't want for shit and neither will my wife and kids. I looked at him and knew I wanted to be a better man.

"I understand Roscoe but if something happens to us who is going to take care of the kids. Journey isn't old enough and Haven is only twelve."

"Don't worry about that because nothing is happening to us." I sat back on the bed listening to them go back and forth.

My siblings were so scared that we all stayed in my sisters' room. I grabbed my blanket and pillows and went back to her room and went to sleep on the floor. Journey had a full-size bed but I let her and my brother occupy it like I always did.

"Haven come here." I heard my mom try and whisper when she opened the door. I glanced at the bed and Journey and Jax were asleep. I followed her out the door and into their bedroom where my dad was counting money. He never made it out of high school and was taking forever to count it. I just started picking money up and helping. By the time we were finished, I counted out ten thousand dollars for him. I had a smile on my face, but my parents didn't.

"Haven do you know what this is?" My dad asked. I thought it was a trick question.

"Ugh money."

"To you its money. To us this is you, your bother and sisters future. I know you think I'm not giving your mom money or taking care of you the way a man should." I went to say something, but he held his hand up.

"I love all of y'all with every fiber in my body. I know I don't show you kids enough like I should but I'm going to try and change that." I looked at my mom as she smiled at my dads' words.

My mom was a beautiful woman and I saw the way my dad cherished and worshipped the ground she walked on. He was never abusive to her and she had a certain aura about her that could calm the wildest beast down.

She was a white woman with gray eyes that my brother and I inherited while my sister had my dad's hazel eyes. She wasn't your average looking white women because she kept herself up. Men of all races always did a double and triple take when my mom was in their presence. Some would try and offer to take her out and give her money, but she only had eyes for my dad. My dad wouldn't say it but he loved the way my mom loved him.

My dad was tall, dark skinned and weighed at least two hundred and fifty pounds. He had hazel eyes, a goatee and a low-cut fade. Women threw themselves at him and as far as I know he never took the bait. I'm not saying he didn't ever step out on my mom, but I've never heard them argue about another woman and not has one ever approached her. I think he was too scared she would leave him.

"The reason I'm showing you this money is because there's something going on out in these streets and I want to make sure you are taken care of. Tomorrow, I want you to go down to the Verizon store and get three cell phones for you, Journey and Jax."

"Dad I'm only twelve."

"Boy I know that. Grandma is going to take you." My grandma was his mother who we absolutely loved. The only thing is she was a bitch when she didn't have any liquor.

"Ok."

"After you get the phones, I want you to ask them to put a thousand dollars on each account which will count as a credit. That should pay the bill up to a few months. If anything happens, you will at least have a phone." I wasn't sure why he was telling me all this, but I damn sure listened.

"After you get the phone, I want you to go to the mall and buy all of you some summer clothes and sneakers but don't spend more than a thousand dollars on each of you. Last but not least whatever you have left I want you to keep in a safe place."

"What's going on ma?" She came and grabbed my face and wiped my tears.

"WOLF." I jumped when he called me that.

"Wipe those fucking tears. If anything happens to me, you are going to be the man of the house and there's no room for crying. Do you understand me?" He spoke in a firm tone.

"Yes."

"Now give your mom a hug and go to bed." I did what he said and went back to my sisters' room.

"Haven, what did daddy say and why was he yelling? He only calls you Wolf when he's mad. What happened?" My sister questioned me quietly while my brother slept. She and I were very close but not like Jax and I was and that's probably because we were boys. I know you're wondering why they call me Wolf so let me tell you.

My name is Haven, but my dad named me Wolf because of my gray eyes. He said they were scary and resembled a wolf. I have a caramel complexion and I already stood at five foot eleven and I was only twelve. I had perfect teeth, but I had two that always stuck out like fangs.

My dad said since he could remember I would always sneak out the room and peek to see what was going on. No one would ever know I was there. He said it was like I was hunting my prey quietly. I never really paid attention to that until two weeks after that night my parents had the talk with me, I heard a noise coming from downstairs.

I peeked out of my bedroom and notice Journey and Jax were doing the same thing. I made both of them come in my room and had them go in the closet. A year ago, my dad put a hole in there and made it an area for us to hide if anything happened. If you looked in there you wouldn't see anything because the opening to the wall camouflaged.

"But I don't want to go in there." Journey said pouting.

"Just do it." I gave both of them a look and they disappeared.

I cracked the door opened and tiptoed out the room. The way the house was made you could see downstairs from the top of the steps. I was able to see the perpetrators perfectly and I knew exactly who they were.

Dice was some twenty-one-year-old whose father just

passed down the drug empire to him. My dad hated him because he said the power went to his head and he treated people like shit. My dad said his father was ruthless but nothing like Dice.

"You thought I was playing with you motherfucker. Now I'm going to kill you and your entire family."

Phew! Phew! Phew! Phew!

Neither my mom nor dad begged for their life as he pointed his gun and killed them in cold blood.

I ran back in my room and opened up the window to make it seem like we ran out. There was a fire escape outside which made it believable. I heard them come in the room asking where are the fucking kids? *They were really going to kill us too.* You could hear shit being tossed around. The hangers could be heard being moved around letting us know they were in the closet. It was so dark in the wall that I couldn't put my finger up to tell Journey and Jax to be quiet because they wouldn't see me.

We heard what sounded like more voices in the house and stayed where we were. None of us moved and ended up sleeping sitting in that closet. The crazy part about it is once we came out, I looked around the house and it was fucked up. The sun was peeking through the window and when I looked at the clock it was a little after six. I went downstairs and my parents' bodies were gone, and it appeared that nothing ever took place besides maybe a robbery.

"Journey, I want you to lock the door when I leave and Jax you are not to go out this house. Do you two understand me?"

"Where are you going and where is mom and dad?" Jax asked me looking around.

"They're gone. Dice came in and killed them last night" It was no need to sugar coat anything. Journey covered her mouth and I saw one tear leave Jax's eye. He had the same look I did, and he was only ten.

"You already know." I said to him and he nodded his head.

"Make sure you help Journey and I'll be back. There should be some food in the fridge to cook. We have to make sure no one realizes mom and dad are gone. When I get back,

I'm going to call grandma."

"I want them to suffer but I don't want you to get caught. Kill them and get back." Jax said and Journey just stood there staring. I know she was going to take it the hardest because my mom was her best friend and she was daddy's girl even though he barely showed it.

I put a black hoodie on with black pants and grabbed the two hunters' knives my dad had and slid them in my boots. My dad taught me how to throw knives at a young age. I had impeccable skills with that and a gun.

Today would be my first time showing them off. I found some black gloves in my fathers' room and went on my mission. I knew exactly where Dice hung out at and went straight there.

I didn't see him and it was probably because it was early but I sat there behind the dumpster for hours waiting. I noticed it was getting dark and figured he wasn't coming. As I was about to leave, I saw him and the same dude getting out the truck laughing. I pulled the drawstrings as tight as I could to cover my face and walked to where they were but not out in the open for anyone to see me.

"Punk ass motherfuckers." I said loud enough for both of them to hear. I saw the other dude look over where I was. They both started walking towards me and I backed up further to make them come to me.

"Oh shit. It's some little nigga who thinks he tough." The other dude who wasn't Dice said.

"Nah, that's Rosco's son. Where you been nigga? We've been looking for you." He nodded his head to the dude but before he could speak, I threw the knife and it caught him in the throat. His body hit the ground and Dice stared into my eyes.

"You think you tough nigga?" He asked going for his gun. I tossed the other knife at him but threw it at his stomach. The good thing about doing this is, it was springtime and all they were wore t-shirts. Had it been winter this would've been a lot harder. He fell to his knees.

"You think you can come into a man's house and kill him in front of his kids? You fucked with the wrong parents." I said and let two shots off in his head.

I didn't have one of those silencer things, so the shots were loud. I had to get out of there quick. I snatched the knife out of both of their bodies and ran off like a thief in the night. I made a cross against my chest, blew a kiss up to the sky and told my parents to rest in peace. I had avenged their murder and that would be the end of it; or so I thought.

Journey

Present Day

"We have breaking news here on channel 7 news. Cops have found the bodies of a couple over in Englewood NJ with no identification. They are asking the public for help to identify the body. The cops said there was a locket that read, my mom is the best on it. If you or anyone have any information that you can give to the cops to help, please contact the Englewood police department." The newscaster said two days after our parents were killed. My grandmother looked at me and I had tears coming down my eyes.

She jumped up, called the police department and told them she thinks that's her son and was on her way to identify him. Unfortunately, she wouldn't allow us to go thinking it would traumatize us and I'm glad she didn't. I refused to see my parents like that. It was ten years ago to the day and I still had that memory in my head.

Today was my first day back to college from summer vacation. I was finishing up my master's in child psychology and couldn't wait to graduate in May. I had an internship at one of the local offices.

I was able to sit in on the discussions and some of the kids had a lot more issues than I did. The last day of my internship the head Psychologist called me in her office and offered me a position the same day I graduate in May. I was so happy that my brother Haven took me out with his then fuck buddy Candy to celebrate.

My grandmother hated her, and she was never afraid to say it. Haven always thought the shit was funny and would laugh in Candy's face where I thought it was rude as hell. I always asked my brother how would he feel if some guy did that to me? He would always say, *ain't no nigga that stupid.* I swear he gets on my nerves, but I love him to death.

I parked in the student section at the college and grabbed all my things before I got out the car. I hit the alarm and headed towards the psychology building a few minutes early so I wouldn't be late for class.

I walked in and there were a few other people who must've thought the same thing because they were in here also.

21

There was one guy who caught my eye, but he was the type that looked too thuggish and my brothers Haven and Jax were enough thugs for me.

"Ms. Banks can you stay after class? I would like to speak with you about something." When he said my name, I noticed the thuggish dude pop his head up and look at me.

"What?" I said to him and stood in front of him.

"What you mean what?" He leaned back in his chair and let his eyes roam my entire body.

Now I may front like I'm not a shy person, but I am very insecure when it comes to my looks. The way he continued staring made me turn and walk away. I made sure my laptop bag was all the way behind me covering my butt that was barely there.

"Yes Professor." I said when I reached his desk. He was looking down at some papers that had my name on them.

"Ms. Banks, I have been looking over your previous grades and you by far have the best ones I've seen in a long time. Have you ever received a grade lower than an A minus?" I chuckled and put my head down.

22

"No sir. I take my education very serious."

"I see that. Listen, I put an ad down in the student center because I need a student teacher this semester and I was wondering if you would be interested."

"Oh my God really. Of course, I would be interested. When would I start?" I was acting like a kid that just got a new toy.

"Calm down Ms. Banks. There is an interview process with the Dean and me, but I don't see that being a problem. However, you will need to be on time and dress as if you are the professor. Some days I will send you the lesson plan on a Friday and expect you to teach the following Monday. I also need your schedule so the days you don't have class you can student teach in my other ones."

"Thank you so much. I swear you won't regret this."

"I'm sure I won't Ms. Banks. I've heard nothing but good things about you." I gave him a look and he just smiled. I didn't even bother to ask him to elaborate. I was floating on cloud nine and didn't want to come down. I grabbed all my things and headed out the door. It was a little after eleven and my next class wasn't until one. I decided to grab something to eat out the cafeteria.

"Oh my goodness. I'm sorry. I didn't mean to bump into you." I said picking up my notebook and purse that fell without looking up.

"Its all good ma. I see you're about to be my teacher on certain days." He said. I turned around and it was the same man who was in the class staring at me.

I took in his appearance and I can't lie, this man was FINE. If he weren't standing there, I would be fanning myself. He was may be six foot one with brown eyes and deep waves in his hair. He was brown skinned and had muscles coming out his t-shirt. He was Versace down to his sneakers. I mean even his book bag and the shades on top of his head were Versace. I only knew this because Haven wore the same type of clothing. He said if a man couldn't afford to wear expensive things then he didn't deserve a good woman. I don't know why he had that mentality being we were never rich but that was Haven for you.

"First off, I'm not your ma and when you address me you can at least call me by my first name." I said snapping on him for no reason at all.

"Calm down. I was trying to be nice. You snapping on a nigga for no reason."

"Look, I'm sorry. I just got some great news as I can tell you already know from listening and I wanted to get something to eat. I get cranky when I'm hungry so again I apologize." I said and he smiled showing off the deepest dimple on his right cheek. I've never seen a dimple so far in that it looks like someone pushed into it.

"It's all good. What you want to eat?"

"Ugh, I'm going to the cafeteria."

"The cafeteria. Don't tell me you eat that nasty shit? Come on you have to let me take you out."

"The cafeteria food is not nasty, and I don't know you to go out with you like that. If you'll excuse me?" I walked away from him fast as hell. I wanted to look back, but I didn't want him to see me doing it.

Once I got to the cafeteria, I turned around and he was nowhere in sight. I found something to eat and sat in a spot by one of the windows. I turned my laptop on and picked up the campus WIFI to look up houses. My brother Jax was coming home in two months and Haven had been asking me to find him a place. I don't know why when both of us had more than enough space at our houses.

"Yes grandmother." I answered the phone and blew my breath out. I loved her but sometimes she was a pain in the ass. Not only did she live with me but being an alcoholic, she stayed drinking at the bars, and I was always stuck going to get her. Haven said I should get her, her own apartment but I don't want to be alone in that big house by myself.

When my parents died my grandmother took care of us like we knew she would. She got a check for each of us once a month from social security since my mom worked. It wasn't a lot, but it was enough.

Anyway, Haven stayed in school, but the streets ended up finding him. He finished high school and graduated top of his class but he didn't go to college. He said my dad always

26

amounts of money into the bank at a time so it wouldn't look suspicious and to find a business to open up as well.

Here we are four years later with a liquor store, two hair stores, and a beauty salon that I go to once a month to get my hair done and check the books. I hated going into that place because it was nothing but gossip.

Haven made a strip club named Jax so when he came home, he had a business and wouldn't have a problem depositing his money in the bank. We walked in the lawyer's office broke; well Haven had a little money hustling and walked out millionaires. I guess that's why my dad was always tight with his money but where did he get six million dollars from was the question?

"Look Heffa. I just wanted to tell you that pain in the ass nigga Maurice came by again looking for you."

"Grandma did you tell him I said it was over and I'm not taking him back this time?"

Maurice was my ex that I had been dating for the last five months. He was a handsome guy and worked at Verizon. He made great money and was very well off. The only thing was he couldn't keep his dick in his pants. You see I'm a virgin and he can't seem to wait until I'm ready, therefore getting it elsewhere. The problem with that is, the person he got it from was in one of the cycling classes at the gym. She and her friend had an entire conversation about how he screwed the daylights out of her. I don't know how she knew who I was but every time she spoke of him, she looked at me.

"Yes, I told him, but you know he tried that crying shit. I had to smack him on the back of the head and tell him to leave before I got my gun out." I started laughing. My grandmother loved Madea and Big Momma movies. It was funny because she'd act like them from time to time.

"Good. Hopefully he'll get the hint."

"Child please. You're a virgin and he knows it. He's trying to be your first so you can be strung out on him. That way when he cheats again you won't leave him. That nigga ain't slick. Girl grandma got your back." I couldn't do anything but shake my head and laugh.

"I know you do. Do you need anything while I'm out? Before you tell me, just know tonight I will be late because it's the day I go to the shop to get my hair done and do the books."

"No, I'm ok. Drive safe and I'll see you when you get here. Love you Journey."

"I love you too grandma."

The rest of the day seemed to fly by. I left the library around five and headed over to the shop to get my hair done and make sure the books were good. I don't care what Haven said, I was surely about to put an ad out for a bookkeeper. That way the person could do the books at all the businesses.

I parked in the owners' parking space and went in. As usual it was crowded but my girl Venus was waiting for me like always.

"Hey boo." She said and waved me over.

"What's up girl?" I put my purse on her counter and sat down. She wrapped the cape around my neck and parted my hair to get ready for the perm. I was mixed and had long hair, but it was thick and the only way to tame it was with a perm.

"Listen, my brother is having a get together at his house and I want you to come."

"I don't know Venus. I have to go over the books and I'm not usually done until late. Then, I just started classes today so I have…" She put her hand up and cut me off.

"How long have I known you?" She asked applying the perm.

"I don't know four maybe five years why?"

"Exactly. So I know when your ass is coming up with an excuse. You always have me at your house, and we do things you want to do. Anytime I ask you to do something with me you always have an excuse. I didn't want to say anything, but that shit is pissing me off. Now I'm going to finish your hair and send you home. Those books aren't going anywhere, and you can do them tomorrow." I went to say something, and she gave me a look not to say anything.

"Venus, I don't have anything to wear."

"Bitch bye. I've been in your closet and its shit in there with tags still on them; including shoes." I didn't say anything else because she was right.

I met Venus one day in the coffee shop going off on someone when we bumped into each other. We both said sorry but then the next two days we kept ending up at the same place at the same time.

Eventually, we sat down and had a conversation. I learned she was a hairdresser looking for work because her dad cut her off. Since we were about to open the shop, I interviewed her right there. She brought me her certificates and other credentials and now she runs the shop for me. I love her like she was my sister and I think she felt the same.

I got home from the shop and my grandmother was entertaining her old ass boyfriend. Don't get me wrong he was nice and loved my grandmother, but I hated when I heard them having sex. Both of them sounded like cats getting run over or some shit. I spoke to both of them and ran upstairs to find something to wear.

Two hours later I was dressed in a dark blue mid length dress that had a small split up the back. I had on some silver strap up sandals with silver jewelry to match. I didn't have a big chest, so I wore a push up bra to show a little bit of cleavage since the dress required it. I let my hair down and smiled at myself in the mirror. I may not have a banging ass body, but I will always flaunt what my momma gave me.

"You look gorgeous Journey and I'm happy you're going out. Now don't come back too early."

"Why not?"

"You know its Friday and I like riding my man's dick on Fridays." I pretended like I was gagging in my hand.

"That was too much for my young ears grandma."

"Where the hell you going?" Haven asked walking up on the porch.

"To hang out with Venus."

"Oh ok. You look pretty sis. Be safe and I love you." He said and kissed my cheek.

On Fridays him and a few of his boys would come by my house and play cards with my grandma and her man until about eleven. My family may be small, but we stuck together. I don't how long they planned on being there tonight if Grams just said she was trying to get it in.

****

33

"Hey. I'm outside." I spoke in the phone to Venus when I pulled up to some huge ass mansion. I handed my keys to the valet and walked to her.

"Damn sis. You look beautiful."

"Girl, you've seen me dressed before."

"Yea but not with your hair down and dressed like you going out on a date. Usually you throw your hair in a ponytail when we go out for drinks and you're never in the club."

"Do you think its too much?"

"No. And don't let anyone tell you different." She stopped and turned around.

"Before we go in let me tell you a few things." I gave her a crazy look.

"My brother can be ignorant as hell and his fake ass girlfriend is going to be deathly jealous of you. Don't pay it any mind. She's ugly and anyone that looks better than her is on her shit list. You'll know if she's hating because she'll stand in the corner by herself staring at you. As far as the other women here, trust me they're here trying to catch a baller."

"I assume your brother is in the business." She nodded her head and we walked in. She didn't have to tell me anymore than that. Hell, my brother was in the same business, who was I to judge.

I stepped in the house and Venus left me there to go get her brother. She wanted to introduce us. I glanced around the house and to say it was anything less than magnificent would be a lie. Everything about it screamed drug dealer or kingpin.

"Colby, this is my friend Journey that I've been telling you about." I could hear her speaking, but I was taking a wine glass off the waiters' tray.

"I can't wait to meet the woman who Venus has been claiming as her sister." I turned around and there he was looking fine as ever with a smirk on his face.

Colby

I noticed her when she walked in, but I wasn't sure who she came with. I saw my sister talking to her, but my sister talked to everyone except Willow who is my on and off again girlfriend. Those two hated each other.

Willow had a hand problem and I had to let Venus dig in her ass a few times because I didn't hit women. I let my eyes roam Journey's body and I have to say I was impressed. She put her head down and started blushing when I licked my lips. I had that effect on women all the time.

She sipped the wine and grabbed another one from the waiter who had come back around just that fast. Venus looked from me to her a few times and started grinning.

"Ugh, I'm going to assume you two met."

"Something like that." I said and extended my hand out. She placed the glass in her right hand to shake mine with the left.

"Nice to meet you Journey Banks."

"How do you know her last name?"

"We have a class together." I told Venus who was being nosy as hell.

"How are you Colby?" My sister looked at me.

"Oh, I'm sorry. It's Colby Foster." She corrected herself for some reason. I lifted her hand to kiss it and again she blushed.

"Let me show you around before my brother has your panties pushed to the side with his dick inside you." Journey let her mouth fall open when she said that. I shook my head laughing because my sister knew me too well.

"Yo, who the hell was that?" My brother Wesley asked. He and I were brothers but had different moms. We both worked for my dad.

"Someone pops wants me to get close to."

"Damn. I wish he would've asked me."

"Nigga please. You wouldn't know what to do with a classy woman like that. That's why he sent me after her and not you."

"Touché nigga but be careful. If he sent you for her there's a reason and by the way you're staring at her she may have the power to make you fall in love." I heard him speaking but I wasn't listening.

"Nah. I don't know why he wants me to get next to her, but it has to be a reason."

"You think he wants you to kill her?" He asked as we both continued to stare in her direction.

"I don't know but if he does shit happens." I walked over to where Willow stood and stalked my prey as she went outside with my sister. If I was in the presence of my girl, she wouldn't cut a fool and I don't need her acting up. That would only scare Journey away and I couldn't have that.

I spent most of the night mingling with everyone there except the one I wanted to. I admit Journey was a beautiful woman and I wouldn't mind getting to know her.

However, I had to keep the relationship platonic and remain focused on the task. I saw her coming in with Venus and noticed Willow standing in the corner with hate in her eyes. I have no idea why that woman hated the world. She didn't want any chick near me and if Venus wasn't my sister it would be no different for her.

"I just wanted to tell you I had a great night. Thanks for allowing me to come." Journey said as she walked past me. I saw Willow staring but I gave her a look that she better not start any shit.

"Why you leaving so soon?" She glanced down at her phone.

"Colby it's after two in the morning an I'm tired."

"Well can I at least get your number before you go?"

"Ugh, I don't think she will like that." He pointed over to Willow who was standing there with her arms folded.

"She'll be alright." I waved Willow off.

"Look Colby. You seem like a nice guy but I'm not some woman who falls over a man for his good looks or money. You are very charming but you have a woman and I'm not the disrespectful or side chick type. Thanks again for a great night."

"Oh shit bro. It's a first time for everything." Wesley said behind me.

We watched her get into her white 2016 Cadillac CTS truck. She pulled off and I made a mental note of her license plate. I see she was going to play hard to get and if I didn't want to piss my pops off, I had to do whatever it took to get her.

I hit my boy up and asked him to find the address of the plates so I could send some flowers to her.

"Yup. But I can bet a few more times with this playa and she'll be dropping those panties just like the rest of them."

"Playa. Playa." We both said at the same time.

"Aren't you leaving Wesley?" Willow asked and wrapped her arms around my waist.

"Yo, when are you going to get rid of this killjoy? I swear she'll make a nigga want to commit suicide just by being around her. You could be having a good time and here comes Willow to kill it with that face and attitude. Fuck outta here."

"Fuck you Wesley."

"No thanks. My brother and I don't share. I'm out bro before she fucks my high up. If I were you, I would go straight to bed to avoid sex with her. Yuk, man how do you do it?"

"Alright Wesley take your drunk and high ass home." I motioned for Venus to come get him. I know he was drunk, and I also knew he hated Willow too.

"Call me when you make it home sis." I kissed Venus on the cheek.

"Bye Venus." Willow said sarcastically.

"Ugh ah bitch you tried it. You know I don't like you so stop acting like I do in front of my brother. You still have him. For now." She threw in there and winked as she stepped off the porch.

Willow slammed the door and went upstairs talking shit. I locked up and followed suit. I wasn't in the mood for her shit tonight and I think she knew because she picked her bag up to go home. No she didn't live with me anymore. We did for about a year but then she got caught cheating when I was outta town and tried to say it was because she figured I was. I know it was a dumb ass reason but whatever.

I took her back after a few months of begging but in between I was fucking. At some point in time she had a hand problem. Nothing major but she would smack me when she got mad or sneak me when I was asleep. The last time Venus beat her ass so bad she ended up in the hospital and I left her there.

"I guess you don't care that I'm going home." I continued taking my clothes off and got in the shower. It was just a matter of time before she followed behind me. Like I said the shower door opened and she stepped in and immediately got on her knees.

Willow could suck a mean dick but she hated to swallow which was fine with me but I did miss the feeling from other chicks doing it. Her pussy was good but not excellent and if I had to score her, I would say it was a C plus.

"Swallow that Willow." I said when my nut started cumming out just to see what she would say.

"Hell no nigga. You know I don't like the way it taste."

"Whatever yo. Bend over so I can hit it from the back. The entire time I was hitting it all I could think of was Journey. I know I wasn't shit for thinking about another woman while I was in one.

When it started feeling good, I would shut my eyes and see Journey so I would open them back up. Willow started throwing her ass back and it was feeling too good that I had to open my eyes again to remember who I was fucking.

A few minutes later I pulled out and came on her ass. I was messing up by not using a condom, but you could bet that wouldn't happen again. There's no way I hell I would have a baby with her. She was already crazy, and I didn't need that in my life for the next eighteen years.

****

The weekend flew by and it was Tuesday and time for me to get to the class I had with Journey. She and I had the same psychology class three days a week and today was the first besides last Friday which was really an introduction to the class.

I popped my laptop open and pulled up the assignment we had due. Yes a nigga was in school getting his degree. I observed people, it was what I did for a living and what other way to get better at it then major in psychology?

"Good morning class and welcome. My name is Journey Banks and I will be student teaching with the Professor. Unfortunately, I wasn't supposed to start this soon told him he was the man of the house so even though he went to school by day and hustled by night, he still made sure we had everything.

Once he graduated high school he was contacted by a lawyer. He wasn't sure what was going on and since I was in college for Business, he thought I should go with him.

The day we saw the lawyer he informed us that my dad had a life insurance policy for him and my mom that totaled a million dollars each. He also had stocks and bonds in our names that couldn't be touched until I was twenty-one and he was eighteen which is why we were there. Jax couldn't receive his until he was eighteen as well.

The lawyer locked the door to his office and came in the room with six duffle bags. Now I'm no rocket scientist but you can tell money was in them. By the time he explained everything to us we both had the look of shock on our faces.

We were given two bags each and Jax's bags were put away for when he came home from jail. Each bag contained a million dollars in cash. The lawyer told us to deposit small but he had a family emergency. He sent me the lesson plan and if everyone would open there textbook to Chapter one, we can start there." She said and smiled when she noticed me.

I couldn't help but stare. Journey was not the definition of a bad bitch was she was definitely a gorgeous woman. You could tell she was mixed with something by the light skinned complexion. The hair that she had flowing down her back in a ponytail appeared to be hers and the petite body frame told me she didn't have a big chest or ass. The pencil skirt she wore allowed me to see her well-shaved legs and the red bottoms put some height on her short self. But none of that mattered as I listened to her teach the lesson and answer questions as if she were the professor herself. I couldn't help but wonder what my father wanted with her.

"How did I do Mr. Foster?" She walked up to my seat and stood in front of me. I looked around and the room was vacant besides the two of us.

I stood up and towered over her and she bit down on her lip. I almost bent her ass over the desk by how sexy she looked doing it. I cleared my throat and gave her my thoughts.

"Well Ms. Banks, I have to say I was unsure that you would be able to keep my attention on the lesson and not you. However, you did both and for me that is a hard thing to do."

"Oh really. If you were paying attention to the lesson, then how could you entertain yourself with me?"

"You have no idea." I licked my lips and she moved away and back down to the Professors desk. I followed her and stood over her.

"This is going to happen whether you want it to or not." I pointed to the both of us and moved in closer. I noticed her take a few steps back.

"Mr. Foster, I like that you're confident, but this right here won't happen as long as there is another woman occupying your time." She started gathering her things.

"You may see me as an easy target because I'm shy and stay to myself, but you are sadly mistaken. I demand respect from a man as well as all his time and attention."

"Ok and?"

"A man will have to cater to my every need as I would to his. I want a man that won't be afraid to call me out on my shit without being disrespectful. Last but not least, I need a man that will protect me at all cost no matter what the situation. And when I say protect me at all cost, that means protect me from harm that one may try to bring me, and he has to protect my heart."

"I can do all that but what do you mean protect your heart?"

"That's how I know you're not the man for me." She was in my face.

"You see if you were, you would know that yes my heart is on my body but when a woman falls in love, she literally gives her heart to a man and expects him to cherish and treat it like his own. If her heart hurts, then so does his. He will do anything in the world to make sure that she feels no pain. Good day Mr. Foster." She walked out and left me standing there looking crazy.

As smart as my mouth could get, I had no response to that deep shit she just said. I packed my things up and went to my next class. I sat there in deep thought about the knowledge she just dropped on me. Maybe this was going to be a problem like Wesley said.

Jax

"What up brother?" Wolf said when I got in the front seat of the truck he picked me up in.

"Not a damn thing. Just happy to be coming home and eating some of grandma's food. Tell me she cooked for me."

"Nigga you know she did. You were always her favorite no matter what you did."

"That's true. But you were mommy's favorite and Journey was dads, so I guess we're even." I told him and he shook his head.

It has been five years since I saw the outside of the jail cell and I could honestly say I was not going back. He and I reminisced the entire ride as he drove to what he told me was my new house.

When he parked, I asked him what the house had in it. He said Journey picked it out and to be aware that she decorated it. I'm sure it had a girly touch to it. It was a five bedroom, three and a half baths with a pool and basketball court. There was a two-car garage that I could see, and it was gated. The code was my birthday. I saw cars up and down the street and the driveway had just as many.

I know most of these people were the ones we grew up with but I'm sure some were there for a free BBQ, but I was cool with that. He opened the garage to show me the Porsche and Maserati parked inside. I couldn't wait to drive those bad boys tomorrow or even later on tonight.

He opened the door from the garage and the aroma from the food hit me right away. I looked in some of the trays and there was Jamaican food along with catered food.

"I missed you so much." Journey said, jumped in my arms and started crying. I had to hold my own tears back. I hadn't seen her the whole time I was locked down. I wouldn't allow her to see me in that caged place and I know it took a toll on her. We were always close as kids and the day I got arrested she broke down; that shit killed me.

I was on the block hustling when two dudes came out of nowhere and started shooting. They missed but my ass followed them running down the street. I found one hiding behind a dumpster and shot him in the head but the other one got away.

A few days later I was at the same spot hustling when someone started shooting at me again. I figured it was a hit put out on me, but I didn't know by whom because I stayed to myself. As you can tell the person failed again.

The following week I was coming home, and I had a kilo of dope on me that Wolf told me to take in the house. I was walking up the steps when all these cops ran down on me. When I got arrested, I had the dope on me, a gun and six thousand dollars in cash. Thank goodness Wolf made me throw the gun away I killed the other dude with; otherwise, I would've gotten a murder charge.

They gave me seven years for distribution and unlawful use of a weapon. I was a juvenile, so I was able to get two years knocked off because it was my first charge.

"I missed you too sis." She stayed in my arms hugging me for a few more minutes.

"Get your big ass off my baby." I heard my grandmother yelling. She kissed my cheek and I let her down.

My grandmother gave me a hug and she herself didn't want to let me go. The love I received from them and my brother was enough to show me I needed to get my shit together so I could be around them. I already wasted too many years and I wasn't wasting anymore.

"Come on Jax. I got you some clothes to wear and my friend is here to cut your hair.

Journey pulled me into the downstairs bathroom and some chick was in there with her back turned setting stuff up. When she turned around, I smiled.

"Venus?"

"Jax?"

"Hold up. How do you two know each other?" Journey asked with a confused look on her face.

"Girl this is the dude I told you I was writing in jail. He and I met last year when I went to the prison with Monica. I had no idea he was your brother." Venus and I met one day she was on a visit with some chick and I had some hoe coming up there to fuck.

After the visit, I had dude get her information and wrote her to see if she would respond. When she did, I had her come visit me and she cut my fuck visits off. She had me take everyone off my list except her and family. This chick had my head gone and I didn't even have the pussy yet. She said there was no way our first time would be in a jail and if I wanted to be with her the way I said there should be no problem waiting.

I respected Venus enough not to pressure her. She and I wrote each other at least twice a week and she came for a visit once a week. I can't tell you how many times I wanted to take her behind the vending machine or in the bathroom for a quickie. I didn't care how much time they added. I wanted her in the worst way and for her to be standing here about to cut my hair let me know fate played a huge part in this.

"Why didn't you tell me you were coming home, and Journey why didn't I know this was your brother? This is weird." She said and we all started laughing.

"I was going to surprise you." I told her and she sat on my lap and kissed me.

"I don't know why you didn't know. We have pictures around the house." Journey was still acting weird.

"Yea, but when I come over, I don't pay attention."

"Well that's your fault and get off my brother." Journey was very protective of Wolf and me.

"I'm sorry to tell you Journey but this is my man. He and I made it official what was it three months ago right babe?" I nodded my head. Journey went storming out. I told Venus to finish my hair so I could get dressed and go back to the party. I would deal with my spoiled sister later. When she was finished, I helped her straighten up the bathroom.

"Yo, I'll be back." I told Wolf and headed upstairs to find my room. I had no idea what was what until I opened the door and saw Journey lying on the bed. I could hear her sniffling. I guess this was my room if she was in it. It was decorated in black and silver, the bed was a California king and I couldn't wait to sleep in it.

"What's wrong sis?"

"I feel left out. Why didn't you tell me you had a girlfriend? I mean thank goodness we're friends but..."

"Stop it." I cut her off.

"Journey women come and go but you will always be my sister. Don't ever think you will be in competition with any chick I'm with. To be honest, I'm happy you two know each other. I don't have to worry about you getting along." She wiped her eyes and I pulled her in my arms for a hug.

"I love you sis."

"I love you too."

"Let me get dressed and I'll be down in a few." She nodded her head and opened the door. I removed my clothes and went in the bathroom.

There was a tub on one part and the shower was on the other side. I looked in the small closet and grabbed some shampoo, soap and a rag. I allowed the hot water to beat down on my body as I handled my business in there. I got out, grabbed the towel and wrapped it around my body.

"Your sister told me I could find you here." Venus said lying naked with her legs cocked open playing with herself. I licked my lips and moved in closer. I planned on sexing her later but fuck it. I moved her hand out the way, turned her to face me and pulled her body to the end of the bed. She sat up and removed my towel.

"Damn Jax." She said and wrapped her mouth around my dick.

"Fuck Venus." I moaned out as she had my dick soaking wet from her mouth. I've been away a long time but in all my life I've never encountered someone suck my dick as good as she did. I was happy I jerked myself off in the shower; otherwise, I would've cum as soon as she put me in her mouth.

"Just like that Venus." I grabbed the back of her hair and went in and out her mouth slowly.

When I came, she made sure everything I had was in her mouth. I told her to scoot back on the bed and prayed I remembered how to eat pussy. I'm not saying I couldn't but again jail had a nigga out of service for a while.

I let my tongue slide up and down her slits. Once her pearl started to swell, I attacked it at full force. I put two fingers inside and found her g spot. Shorty was squirting everywhere.

"Jax baby don't stop. Yes, yes yesssssss." She yelled out cumming again for the third time. I stood up and stared at her. Venus was a bad bitch by all means. She reminded me of that Erica Mena chick minus all that ratchetness. I entered her sweet spot and came right away.

"It's ok baby." She whispered in my ear and licked inside and around it. That was my spot and my dick was hard in no time.

I entered her again and this time our tongues were entangled as I pounded her. I pushed her legs back and went deeper making her scream out. The DJ had the music so loud I wasn't worried about anyone hearing her. I had her get on all fours and it was like heaven when she started throwing her ass back. I was ready to cum, but she wanted to get on top.

"Fuck woman. Ride this dick like you promised." She leaned in and kissed me hard before standing up on her feet and riding the shit out of me. I smacked her ass and she screamed out and her juices leaked out from underneath her.

"Ride that shit girl. Yea just like that." She went harder and I could feel my nut coming.

"I love you Jax. Oh my God, I love you." I pumped harder under her as she came again and this time, I came with her. We both laid there not saying a word.

"I love you too Venus."

"Am I your woman?" I looked down at her.

"You know you are. Why would you ask me some crazy shit like that?"

"Jax let's be honest. You just came home from a bid and I know we were pen pals. If you wanna fuck with other chicks to catch up on what you missed then I'll back up. I don't want to get myself caught up in any drama because you wanna experience other women."

"I'm good on other women babe. I'm not going to lie and say I won't be at a strip club because I own one. But just know everyone will know you're my woman and you can come there anytime you want without being worried about catching me out there. I'm not my brother. If I tell you I love you and you're my woman I mean it. As long as you ride for me, I'll ride for you."

"I'll ride for you baby. I just wanted to make sure we were on the same page. You think I can ride this dick again?" She asked and went down to wake me back up.

"As much as you want, it's yours." Once I said that she went crazy sucking my dick. She had me in the room moaning a few times by how good it was.

We were in the middle of fucking when Journey came banging on the door telling us to stop and save it for later because everyone was looking for me.

"Come take a shower with me." I grabbed her hand and took her with me. After the two of us got dressed we went downstairs holding hands and ran into my worst nightmare.

"What the fuck Jax? You come home and I don't hear from you." This old bitch I fucked with yelled out.

"Move the fuck on Penny."

"Oh, it wasn't move the fuck on when I was fucking you at the jail last week." I felt Venus let my hand go and watched her run out the house.

"Yo, get the fuck out of here. Why would you come in here talking that bullshit?"

"Jax, you said we would be together when you came home." Penny was the fuck buddy I cut off at the jail when Venus and I got serious.

"Yea, maybe to fuck. You know she's my girl and has been for a while. You came in here being messy and all you did was look stupid." I pushed passed her and ran out the house to see if I could catch Venus.

Yea, I fucked Penny, but it was before I made it official with Venus. I didn't expect to see her here or for her to open her mouth, but a jealous bitch will do anything.

"What happened?" Journey asked when she came outside. I told her and she instantly caught an attitude.

"Jax if you're not ready to be committed leave Venus alone. I love her like a sister. She is a good person and has a good heart." She walked away from me.

I couldn't go to her house because my car was blocked in. I guess the only thing I could do was enjoy the rest of the time left of this BBQ and go see her tomorrow. Maybe she'll be calm by then.

Wolf

This is exactly why a nigga didn't have a main chick. I watched Penny go up to my brother and his girl with that bullshit ass lie just to get under Venus skin. I knew the two of them were together. Hell, if you ask me, I think Jax was in love with Venus.

The way he spoke about her when I visited and had me have someone watching her over the last few months, I knew it then. Jax was the lover out of the two of us. When he loved, he loved hard and he never cheated on his girls.

Jax went to jail at the age of fifteen because he was set up by who; we still don't know. He had a little girlfriend back then, but it was nothing but puppy love. Don't get me wrong my brother really loved her too and she would write him but after two years she went started to show her ass. She was fucking any and everybody and the hood called her Penny. Yup the same one who just came in here being shady.

"Get your stupid ass out of here. The fuck you come in here lying for?" I grabbed her arm and pushed her towards the door. She turned around to say something.

"Wolf, you know Jax and I have history. We still love each other and…"

"Bitch he don't love the hoes. Don't bring your ass back over here either. Matter of fact how the hell you even know about this? You know what never mind. Beat your feet before I help you."

"Fuck your Wolf."

Phew. Phew.

I let two shots off with one hitting her in the leg and the other one just missing her head. If anyone knew me, I hated for them to say fuck you to me. Tears were coming down her face.

"Oh my God Wolf, you shot me." I walked up on her as she laid there screaming for someone to help her.

"The next time I say keep it moving do what the fuck I say. I don't like repeating myself and remember who you're talking to. I'm not these fuck niggas you can disrespect. I'll snatch your life right out of your body and still go to the strip club like it never happened." She stared at me covering her mouth. I saw fear written across her face.

"Aye yo. Come drop this stupid bitch off at the hospital." I told my boy Drew.

"That bitch is not bleeding in my car."

"Man, I'll pay for your car to get cleaned. Hurry up before my grandmother comes out here. Just so you know I'm blaming your ass."

"Aw hell no. The last time you blamed me for some shit your grams wouldn't let me eat her cooking for a month. I ain't fucking with you Wolf. Bitch get up." He yelled at Penny.

"I can't. He shot me."

"Who shot you?" I asked with my gun pointed at her head.

"No one. I don't know what happened." She said and put her head down.

"Remember what I said." I told her. Drew held his arm out for her to use him as a crutch, but he moved it when she stood. When she hit the floor, Drew was hysterical cracking up.

"Man stop playing and get her out of here. That's your ass if grams catch you." My grandmother knew what we did but I tried to keep it away from her.

"Alright, alright. Come on." He finally put her in his car.

"Oh yea. Don't think we won't be watching you. Keep your mouth closed or that cute little son you have won't make it to Christmas." I threw up the peace sign and left her with Drew.

I walked in the house and Journey was sitting in the living room with books and her laptop on the couch. Who the hell does school work in the middle of a BBQ? My nerdy ass sister that's who.

I plopped down on the couch next to her. She rolled her eyes at me, so I snatched her reading glasses off her eyes.

"Haven give me my glasses. GRANDMA!" She screamed out and I mushed her in the head.

Journey was my heart, and no one could ever change that. My mom was the first woman I loved, and Journey was the second. And no, I'm not talking about any incest type of shit. I'm talking about the type of love that will have me kill anyone for fucking with them. I'm a savage ass nigga and nothing bothers me except the thought of someone hurting her.

I love my brother and grams just as much, but Journey reminds me so much of my mom. Very laid back, she won't let you disrespect her, and she's not ratchet either. She resembled my mom so much besides the eyes that I can't help but be overprotective of her the way I am. Shit if you think I'm bad, Jax is ten times worse when it comes to her.

Before he went to jail, she wasn't even allowed to say hi to any of our friends nor was she allowed out the house and she was older than both of us. I think he was scared of something happening to her too.

"What did I tell you about saying my real name?"

"Then give me back my glasses." She pushed me on the shoulder and snatched them out my hand.

"Why are you in here?"

"Penny made Venus leave with that nonsense and Jax won't let me outside. He said it's too many niggas out there."

"Get ready for it sis. You know Jax ain't about to let you out of his sight."

"I know. I just wish he gets over it. I can't help that I look just like mommy. I'm not out in the streets like some hood rat and nothing is going to happen to me." I leaned back on the couch listening to her. I understood where she was coming from, but I don't think she understood how deadly these streets are. They care about no one.

"Sis, Jax missed five years of our life; his life. He's not trying to control you but he wants to make sure you stay safe. You know we love you and if anything ever happened to you…" She put her hand up.

"Nothing is going to happen to me." She said. I knew she was oblivious to what was going on and it's going to stay that way.

"Journey take your ass home. It's getting late and I don't want you driving." Jax came on the living room talking shit.

"I'm staying here tonight. Is that ok?" I just laughed. She complained about him being tough on her and she was staying the night.

"That's fine. Everybody is leaving and we're going to the strip club.?" Journey turned her face up.

"What?"

"Jax you were just with Venus."

"Journey I'm not going there to fuck." She gave him the side eye.

"You're right. I was just with Venus and she gave me more than enough to keep me from straying. I know that dumb shit Penny said hurt her but that's still my girl and I wouldn't cheat on her."

"Awww. I want my man to be just like you."

"What man?" We both asked at the same time and she jumped.

"She ain't got no man. Can't none of these niggas appreciate a good woman who still has her in innocence." My grams came in yelling.

"Grams. They do not need to know that."

"You still a virgin sis?" I asked and she put her head down. Her face was beet red.

"Yes." She said quietly.

"Word. That's good Journey. I'm proud of you." Jax told her and went to sit by her.

"Thanks, and before either of you ask. I thought I found the right person, but he couldn't wait for me and was dipping in and out of women."

"Who is he"

"It doesn't matter."

"It's some nigga that keeps coming by the house crying some fake ass tears. I told her he just wants to string her out. I bet his dick little as hell too." My grandmother said making us all laugh.

After everyone left and we made sure grams and Journey locked up before we headed to the strip Club Jax. I named it after him.

"Damn it's some bad ass strippers in here and is it always this packed." Jax asked as Drew and I made our way to VIP. I handed Jax some keys and told him they were to the club, his office and a bunch of other shit I would inform him of later.

"Every weekend. During the week you have the office people who come in here, but the weekends is made for niggas like us." Drew said pulling one of the strippers down on his lap.

"Can I give you a dance daddy?" The stripper asked Jax. I lit my blunt and waited for Candy to bring her ass out. She was my fuck buddy and a stripper.

"HELL NO YOU CAN'T." We all snapped our neck and Venus was standing there with Journey who had her face turned up. This was not my sisters' atmosphere and I was mad as hell she was here and so was Jax.

"Yo what the fuck are you doing here?" I asked Journey. Jax had to deal with his chick.

"Who are you?" The stripper asked Venus.

"This is my woman and she's my sister. When you see them you will show them the upmost respect. If I hear you or any other chick in here did otherwise, I don't think I need to elaborate on what will happen. Journey take your ass upstairs in my office." He handed her the keys and I nodded at Drew. He followed behind her to make sure she went.

"Venus I'm only going to say this once."

"What?" She had her arms folded as if it's his fault the stripper asked for a dance.

"I know you and my sister are close but don't ever bring her to this type of environment again. Do I make myself clear?"

"But she…"

"Do I make myself clear?" He asked giving her a face that would make any chick nervous. Venus nodded and he pulled her in and kissed her. Yea, that nigga was in love but I'm glad he checked his girl because I would hate to have to.

"What are you doing here?" I heard Jax ask her. Shit I was shocked myself since she stormed out the house.

"Journey called and explained what happened with Penny. I'm sorry I didn't allow you to clear your name."

"Damn it's that easy. Maybe I should get me a main chick." I saw some badass woman walking towards me.

"Really." Venus asked me. Everyone wanted me to get a real girlfriend, but I was taking my time.

"Nah. I changed my mind." The woman sat on my lap and had my dick brick hard. Too bad for Candy.

I grabbed shorty's hand and took her in one of the private rooms. I wasted no time lowering my jeans and boxer's half way down and stood there. She got down on her knees and took me in her mouth. The shit felt good as hell but I wanted some pussy. I pumped harder in her mouth until I came. She backed up and didn't swallow.

"Bitch if I knew you didn't swallow, I wouldn't have wasted my time." She rolled her eyes and got up.

I grabbed the condom out my pocket and slid right in. The bitch was tight but not enough where it would make me want to cum fast. Her walls were there but you can tell she's been around. Her pussy was ok and I was ready to nut.

"Shit Wolf. This dick is good as hell." My eyes popped open when she said my name. I continued hitting it from the back for a few minutes then pulled out and came in the condom. I removed the condom and flushed it down the toilet. Yea I had a small bathroom in all the private rooms. Bitches needed to clean there pussy before they went back out there, and niggas had to make sure bitches weren't stealing their cum out the condom from the trash.

"How did you know who I was?" I asked her.

"What?"

"You heard me. Who the fuck sent you?"

"I'm sorry."

"Who sent you?" I questioned because if she's here it

meant someone sent her.

"Freedom."

"Freedom?" *Who the fuck is a Freedom?* I thought to myself.

"Yes he paid me to sleep with you so he could…" I didn't even let her finish and blew her brains out.

I ran out to find my brother and saw four men walking in looking suspect. Jax made eye contact with me and I saw Venus running up the steps. Drew and Jax were headed in my direction but it was too late. Gunfire erupted throughout the club. People were screaming and running. I wasn't worried about anyone but Journey and Jax. I glanced around the club and one of the dudes I saw was aiming his gun at me, but I caught him in the stomach.

"Tell Freedom I'm coming for him." I said in his ear. I didn't want to kill him because I needed him to relay that message. I ran up to the office and my sister was crying and jumped in my arms. Jax came in and he was pissed when he saw Journey.

"Go out the back and take her home."

"I'm sorry Jax. I would've never brought her if…"

"JUST TAKE HER HOME! NOW!" He yelled and Venus jumped. I hope she was ready to be with him. Jax had a bad temper and this shooting was about to bring out the savage in him.

"I'm not leaving until you two leave." Journey cried.

"Journey we're fine. Those dudes are dead. Go home." I walked them down the steps and out the back door.

"I'm sorry Wolf." Venus had tears coming down her face.

"I know Venus. I'll talk to him, but you have to understand he just came home and if anything happened to Journey he would go crazy. It doesn't mean he wants anything to happen to you but we are all we got."

"I know." She rolled the window back up and pulled off.

Colby

"How the fuck did this happen?" I heard my pops yelling when I stepped in his house. I wasn't sure what went down but whatever it was must've been bad if he called a meeting at eight in the morning. He never wanted to see people before ten.

"Yo. You heard what went down last night at Club Jax?" Wesley asked when he came in behind me drinking a damn iced coffee.

"Bro really. You had time to stop at Dunkin Donuts and didn't bring me shit? You selfish as fuck yo."

"Nigga please. Remember that time when you broke up with Willow and had that threesome in your room. You refused to share those bitches." I looked at him like he was crazy.

"Don't look at me like that. Those bitches were bad and I never got over that shit."

"You childish as hell."

"Call me what you want but this iced coffee good as hell." He said sipping through the straw looking at me laughing.

"Are my two sons going to stand outside all morning bitching about some coffee or find out who killed some of my people while their sister was there." That made both of us interested.

"What you mean Venus was there when you sent someone to shoot up some club for whatever reason?" I asked mad as hell.

"Oh I see. You think because I'm keeping you in the dark about some things, that this doesn't concern you unless your sister is involved?"

"Honestly pops that's exactly it. You got Colby and I out here blind trying to get at people. Then you cut our sister off to fend for herself. But you wanna pretend like you were worried that she was in the club you sent someone to shoot up." My pops was mad as hell Wesley talked back to him in front of people.

"Everybody out." My father yelled and at the same time my phone was going off non-stop. I looked down and it was Willow. I'm sure she wanted to argue about me fucking her and sleeping in the guest room. I didn't do it on purpose, but I was feeling crazy lying next to her with Journey on my mind. I walked out to answer the phone.

"What's up?" She started saying something, but I couldn't understand her through the crying. I had to tell her to calm down.

"Colby someone shot my sister in the head last night at Club Jax. She's dead." I ran my hand down my face. I know how tight the two of them were, so I know she was hurting. I had to find out what all happened and why was her sister killed. I went back in the room with my dad and Wesley who were going back and forth.

"Pops what's going on? That was Willow and she said her sister was killed in the club." Wesley looked at me and sucked his teeth. He didn't care for my girl, but he slept with her sister a few times.

"The dumb bitch didn't do her job right. If she had, she wouldn't be dead. Sorry to say she was a casualty of war."

"War? What the hell are you talking about?" I was over my father talking in riddles.

He started explaining how he had been sleeping with

my girls' sister and she was so desperate to help him, she basically went on a suicide mission. My mother was probably turning in her grave listening to him go on and on. Willow's sister was only twenty-three and he was fifty-one. Both of them were bugging.

"Pops that's nasty." Wesley said showing the disgust on his face.

"What's nasty? The fact that she's dead or the fact we were both fucking her? Too bad she doesn't swallow though." He said and Wesley walked out shaking his head.

"Yo, I'm tired of asking what the hell is going on. Either you're going to tell me or I'm backing out of this shit." He sat down in his chair and lit a cigar.

"In due time son you'll see that all of this has a reason." I scoffed up a laugh and walked out.

I hopped in my car with no destination in mind. I heard my phone go off with a notification and it just so happen to pop up with the information I had been waiting on.

I stopped by the flower shop, picked up a dozen lilies and headed to her house. I parked in the driveway and checked the address to make sure I was at the right place. The house was almost as big as mine. I'm not sure what her parents did but she was definitely living comfortably.

"Good morning is Journey here?" I asked the older woman who was standing at the door with a smirk on her face. She didn't look to be any older than forty-five, but she could be older.

"Who you and why are you looking for my granddaughter. She ain't giving up the pussy to you so I suggest you go." I busted out laughing.

"Grandma who are you talking to like that?" The door was opened wider and Journey stood there staring at me like she was in shock.

She had on a pair of shorts that looked too small and a tank top I could see her brown nipples through because she wasn't wearing a bra. She must've saw me looking because she closed her robe.

"Who this nigga Journey?" Her grandmother was standing there leaning on the door smoking a cigarette.

"Grandma he's in one of my classes and can you put

77

some clothes on?" Journey asked and that made me look at her. For her to be an older woman she had a decent body. All she had on was a long shirt that came to her knees.

"Shit, you need to put some clothes on heffa. And don't be looking at my ass when I walk away nigga." Journey went to close the door and I tried to look around her to be smart.

"Really Mr. Foster? My grandmother, and what are you doing here? How did you find out where I live?" I handed her the flowers and kissed her on the cheek.

"Your grandma may be cute, but you're who I want. As far as finding out where you live, I have my ways." We walked off the porch and on the side of the house where there were a few lawn chairs and a patio set. I could see in her face that something was bothering her.

"Are you ok? You don't look like your normal nerdy self." I joked.

"Whatever." She waved me off.

"You sure?" I asked again.

"Yea, I'm fine. I went out last night, there was a shooting and a woman was killed along with some other people." That shit rang a bell in my head as soon as the words left her mouth. My dad had just told us about it. I wanted to see if she knew anything.

"What? I didn't know you hung out at clubs and it's good to see you weren't hurt."

"I don't go out like that. I was with your sister and..." She stopped midsentence.

"And what? Is my sister ok?" I asked standing up about to leave.

"Oh, I'm sorry. Yes, she's fine. I was saying I went with her, but I wasn't about to tell you why. I'm not into telling people's business or that gossiping. It gets too messy and I hate drama." I felt relieved when she told me my sister was ok.

I would personally take my pops out if something happened to her. I think he knew too, that's why he tried to make it seem like he wanted to get at whoever shot in the club. It had nothing to do with Venus but all of whatever he was hiding.

"That's good to know because when you're mine, I don't want anyone in our business." I moved the strands of hair coming down her face and moved closer to her.

"When I'm yours? I already told you Mr. Foster that we will…" I pressed my lips against hers and they were soft just like I expected. She allowed me to separate her lips with my tongue and dance with hers. I felt myself getting hard just from her kiss and tried to stop but I couldn't. Her kiss was addicting, and I couldn't; no, I didn't want to stop.

"Uhmmm, that was unexpected." She said when she found the strength to pull herself away.

"It was but I enjoyed it." I had her stand up and sit on my lap facing me.

"Mr. Foster what are you doing?" She looked down at me. The two of us had been flirting every time we saw each other in class. This was the first time we were alone, and I was taking advantage of it

"Stop calling me that. You know my name is Colby and I'm doing what I want." She leaned in close and our lips met again but this time I heard a soft moan escape from her.

I sucked on her bottom lip and moved down to her neck. She smelled like vanilla and the shit turned me on even more. I moved her hips around my lap and dry fucked her a little from the bottom. I wanted her in the worst way and my dick was mad at me for getting him here knowing nothing was going to happen.

"It feels good Colby." She whispered in my ear as I popped one of her breasts in my mouth.

I placed my hand in her shorts and she was soaking fucking wet. I went to stick my fingers inside to make her cum, but my phone started ringing causing both of us to stop. I looked down and rolled my eyes because it was Willow. I figured she saw the caller as well because she removed herself from my lap, pulled her shirt down and closed her robe. I don't know what this woman was doing to me, but I had to figure it out quick.

"Can I see you later?" I asked standing up fixing myself. She turned her head and I saw the hickey I left on her neck.

"I'm sorry Mr. Foster. I mean Colby but this was a mistake. I should've never allowed it to get this far."

"What do you mean?" I grabbed her hand.

"You have a woman and I was just allowing you to

81

touch my body in places no one has ever been."

"Hold up. Are you a virgin?"

"That's none of your business and I think it's time for you to go." She said pushing me towards the front of the house. I couldn't believe I met a fucking virgin. They were hard to come by now a days, especially at her age.

"It's nothing to be ashamed of if you are." I told her to reassure her its ok.

"Then why did you say it like that?"

"Honestly, a woman as beautiful as you, I would've thought someone took that."

"Are you trying to suggest I'm a hoe?"

"Nah, nothing like that baby."

"Baby? Ok you're doing too much. Goodbye Colby and let's forget this ever happened."

"What's wrong with you?" I stood her in front of me at my car. I lifted her chin and placed another kiss on her soft lips.

"There is nothing wrong with being a virgin. I'm actually happy no one has touched you. I hope you stay like that because I'm coming back for you and that belongs to me."

I kissed her neck and got in my car.

"Goodbye Colby." I stuck the two fingers in my mouth I had playing in her pussy.

"Oh my God. Why did you do that?" She covered her face in embarrassment.

"Don't ever be ashamed that a man wants to savor your flavor. Your pussy taste good as hell from the little sample I got. I can't wait to taste the real thing." She covered her mouth and the expression on her face was funny as hell.

I saw her run in the house and couldn't stop laughing. She may be around my age but her being inexperienced had me very interested.

I called Willow back and listened to her cry and say she needed me. I know I should feel bad but all I wanted to do is go back to Journey. I told her I would be by later because I needed to check on my sister.

"Colby my sister died and you're running around with Venus." Willow cried on the other end of the phone.

"Hold up bitch." I hated that I had to call her out her name but when she spoke like my sister wasn't important, she

83

gave me no choice.

"Venus was there last night and even though she's ok I still need to check on her. Willow, I know this is a bad time for you but don't make me show my true colors."

"I'm sorry Colby. When you finish…" I hung the phone up on her stupid ass. I didn't want to hear shit she had to say.

I pulled up at my sisters' house and text her phone to open the door. When I walked in, I could tell she was still sleep by how tired she looked. Plus, she didn't call me and that's was something all three of us did daily. She closed the door, yawned in my face and I almost smacked her.

"If you don't go brush your teeth before you kill me with that breath, I'ma smack you."

"Whatever Colby. Nobody told you to come this early."

"Early. Venus its eleven o clock."

"Exactly." She sucked her teeth and walked out.

I looked around the house and realized my sister was doing well for herself even though pops cut her off. Wesley and I gave her money, but she would put it in the bank and use her own.

She lived a small three-bedroom ranch house. Her furniture was expensive, and she just got a brand-new car. My sister stayed in the latest fashion and her hair was always done being she was a beautician.

I saw a picture of her and Journey on the table at what looked like the party I had at my house a couple weeks ago. Venus must really love her if she had the picture printed out and put in a frame.

"You like her?" She said scaring the hell out of me and making me knock the frame over.

"Nah, she good people."

"Colby, you know I hate Willow but if you want to pursue Journey, I suggest you drop her."

"Venus she and I…"

"Cut it out Colby. I see it in your face that you have developed more than a friend type of feeling for her. It's the same look you had when you first got with the bitch you with now." My sister was very observant, and she was right.

When I first met Willow, she was the perfect woman.

She had a nice smile; personality and she could suck a mean dick. Never mind that she didn't swallow, just the fact alone she could take all of my ten inches in her mouth was enough to make me keep her around.

Over the years she started changing and I don't know why and at this point I didn't really care. Venus was right about breaking things off with Willow if I wanted Journey.

"You don't see shit." I smiled when I looked back down at the photo.

Journey had this aura about her that made me want to be with her and protect her. She was innocent, inexperienced and smart as hell. Her personality was bubbly like a kid but the way she made you feel like you were just as important as she was, made me look at her different. Maybe I was sent to her for a reason. What? I don't know but God placed her in front of me for something and I'm sure I would find out soon.

"Yea ok. Anyway, what's up?" She said smirking.

"Nothing. I came to check on you. Pops said there was a shooting last night and you were there. Why didn't you call me or Wesley?" She put her knees up to her chin before she spoke.

"I don't know what happened. One minute I was sitting with the guy I mess with and the next thing I know, he's telling me to run upstairs in one of the offices and lock the door. When he came to get me, he yelled at me for bringing Journey."

"Why was Journey there if it's not something she's into and what does Journey have to do with him?"

"You see I was at a BBQ and some chick came in claiming she slept with him. I got mad and left. Journey was at the BBQ with me and stayed behind. She called me up to say the girl lied and told me where my man was. I told her I was going, and she asked could she tag along. I didn't think anything of it, but I should've. Bro.,, You know I can handle shit like that. Journey was a nervous wreck afterwards. She was shaking and babbling about not losing one of her brothers the same way she lost her parents."

"What happened to her parents?"

"I don't know. She doesn't like to talk about it. I tried to get it out of her, but she will shut down or change the subject fast. Whatever happened to them fucked her and her brothers up mentally. If you ask me, I think they witnessed it."

"Damn, that's crazy. I know how it was when mom passed away but she had cancer so we knew it was coming." The shit my sister said made me want to go back and just hold Journey in my arms and tell her I would protect her but could I? I was still with Willow and I am supposed to be getting close to her for a reason.

I stayed at my sisters' house for about an hour talking about a bunch of shit. Willow called me over and over asking when I was coming.

I gave Venus a hug and went to see Willow at her mom's. There were a ton of cars here, so I called my brother up. I didn't get along with some of her peoples and I didn't wanna get caught slipping. He told me he was a few blocks over. I sat in the car smoking and thinking about Journey.

"Nigga, who you thinking about?" Wesley asked hopping in the passenger side and taking the blunt.

"Journey." I looked at him.

"Yo, I don't know what it is about her that has me stuck

but I can't get her out of my head."

"Well you better think quick because here comes that ugly bitch you claim as your woman." We both started laughing. I know I should've corrected him but fuck it. Her time was limited.

"Really Colby? You come here and sit outside smoking."

"Willow get the fuck out of here with that shit. I came to be nice. You know I don't rock with your family so be appreciative I showed up." I noticed she didn't say anything and grabbed my hand. Wesley shook his head laughing. We walked in and I gave her mom and dad a hug. I wasn't even in the house five minutes when shit hit the fan.

"Yo what is these two niggas doing here?" I heard her brother say. I turned around and immediately started bashing his head in with the butt of my gun.

This motherfucker talked shit every time he saw me, and I gave him a pass on the strength of his sister. I heard people yelling but Wesley shut shit down fast as hell. I turned around and saw I had blood on my shoes.

"What the fuck Willow? Get me some paper towels to get this niggas blood off my shoes."

"If you didn't hit him you wouldn't have any on you." I heard another dude say.

"I pointed my gun at him and shot his ass in the shoulder."

"I want someone to say another fucking word and I swear I'm taking everyone in here out." Willow handed me the paper towel and no one said a word.

I wiped my shoes, yanked my girl up by the arm and pushed her out the door. She knew what the hell was going on and they were probably talking shit before I got here.

"That nigga a savage yo. She needs to leave him alone. Who comes in someone's house when they're mourning and does some this shit?" I heard a voice say when we walked out.

"You got some shit with you."

"Colby, I didn't know they would say anything to you. Shit, my sister died and you're over here bugging and…"

"Oh so him talking shit just flew right past you huh? You know what I don't even care. Stay here with your family.

I'm out."

"Colby please don't leave."

"Willow get in here. Outside begging a nigga to stay. You are a weak bitch." I turned around and it was her mom. As long as she didn't pop tough with me, I wasn't saying anything.

"Ma."

"Don't ma me. Your brother and cousin both have to go to the hospital and you're out here worried about him." She slammed the door.

"Am I going to see you later?" She asked and stood on her tippy toes to kiss me.

"Call me when you're on the way over."

"Call you. Since when have I had to do that?"

"Since I may not be home."

"Why don't you just give me the key?"

"Because you're crazy and when I don't want you at my house, I don't have to worry about you sneaking in when I'm sleep. Talk to you later." I kissed her cheek and walked off with Wesley.

"You ain't shit." He said laughing.

"I'm over this relationship with her. I'm going to get through the funeral and then I'm parting ways with her."

"Yea ok. That's what you think. Willow is not letting you go."

"She doesn't have a choice and if she knows what's good for her, she'll walk away without any problems." He nodded his head and went to his car. This was going to be a long ass week.

****

Today Willow asked me to take her to the mall to get an outfit for the funeral. I don't know why when she had clothes at her to wear. We went from store to store until she was able to pick some tight ass black dress that I didn't think was appropriate for a funeral but hey it wasn't mine.

"Can we grab something to eat from the food court?"

"It's going to have to be *to go* because Wesley is waiting for me." She rolled her eyes and I wanted to leave her.

"I'm trying to be nice but you're starting to piss me

off." I tried not to cause a scene.

"Why because I don't like when you leave me for your family?"

"No because you act like I'm not supposed to be with or care about them. You're my girl and yes you come first at times but when they need me then I put them first." She sucked her teeth.

"Yo, get something to eat so we can go. She ordered something from a Cajun place, and we started walking out the door.

"Colby, I miss us. I miss when we used to walk hand in hand and spend time together." I wasn't paying her ass any mind. She grabbed my hand and we stepped out the door. I didn't even know she was standing there until she opened her mouth.

Journey

"Hello Mr. Foster." I said when I saw him and the woman coming out the mall hand in hand. I don't think he was expecting to see me by the expression on his face.

"Oh hey Journey. How are you?"

"I'm good. I see you're still attached." I gave the chick a fake smile.

"Ugh yea you can say that."

"Don't start that shit Colby. You know we're together. I can't stand when one of these want to be model bitches come around and you forget who I am."

"Boo there's no need to get angry. He didn't deny you at all and you're jumping down his throat. It's good to know my classy ass never had a chance with you."

"What's that supposed to mean Journey?" He looked at me with an attitude.

"It means by the looks of it, you have ratchet and ghetto taste but to each his own. See you around." Venus couldn't stop laughing. I may have been strong in front of him but inside my stomach was in knots.

After he left my house that day, he was all I thought about. The way he made my body feel had me go in my room and handle my needs. He hadn't come to class for the following week. He told the professor, he had a death in the family, and I felt bad. Come to find out the chick he's with sister, was the one that got murdered and he was with her.

"She's temporary sis. Trust me, it's you he wants."

"Honestly Venus I don't think I want him." She gave me the side eye.

"I'm serious. He is handsome, charming and a great kisser." I covered my mouth when I said that.

"Oh shit bitch you kissed my brother? When was this and why didn't you tell me? Wait, did you let him break your virginity?"

"No fool and he stopped by the day after the club shooting and brought me flowers. Now that I think of it, I don't know the reason he came by. Anyway, we were talking, he kissed me and that was it. Oh, but his ass left a damn hickey on my neck that I had to cover so my brothers didn't see it." I wasn't going to tell her everything we did.

"You like him?" She said smiling real hard.

"No I don't."

"Yes you do and don't worry he likes you too."

"He told you that?"

"No but he has the same sparkle in his eye when your name comes up just like you do now talking about him. It's ok Journey."

"No it's not. It's not ok for me to be lusting after another woman's man. You know I'm not like that. And who's to say if we got together, he wouldn't get tired of me and do the same thing?"

"No one can answer that. Shit all woman want to know the answer to that question." We both started laughing and continued shopping.

I dropped her off at work and went inside with her to do the books. I finished a little after nine and waited for Venus to lock up. After I saw her pull off, I did the same. I stopped at Walgreens to pick up some Nyquil because I was feeling a cold come on.

"That's the bitch right there I was telling you about." I heard someone say and when I turned around, sure enough it was Colby's girlfriend.

I ignored them and took my items to the cashier. She continued to talk a lot of shit and I let her because my worst fear was getting jumped. I sent Venus a text asking where she was while the lady rung me up. She called me instead of texting back.

"Hey are you around?"

"I'm home why what's up?"

"Oh nothing. I'm at Walgreens and your brother's girlfriend and her friend are talking shit behind me. You know calling me bitches."

"What?"

"I don't have a problem fighting but they're not about to jump me." When she didn't respond I looked at my phone and saw a photo of the sunrise I took at the beach. It was my screensaver. Why did she hang the phone up?

I grabbed my things and walked out the store. I unlocked my door and felt a punch on the side of my face.

I turned around and this chick was in a fighting stance. I tossed my shit in the car and wrapped my hair up. I saw the other chick with her phone out taping us. I didn't care though, I didn't take kindly to a bitch sneaking me.

I hit her in the face making her nose bleed and kept hitting her. She fell on the ground and I started banging her head into it.

"Bitch, I wish you would touch my sister." I knew it was Haven by his voice. I felt someone lift me off the girl and it was Jax. He had me against the car while they checked her out. She was bleeding badly, and I didn't care.

"Take this as a warning." Haven said and knocked the other chick out with one hit. I don't condone men hitting women but she tried to jump me, so she had it coming. I heard a car screech in the parking lot.

"Are you ok?" Venus jumped out and checked me over.

"Yes I'm fine."

"What happened?" Jax asked me.

"Some chicks were talking shit in the store and when I came out, the one I beat up snuck me and well you see how that went. How did you find out?"

"I'm sorry Journey. I wouldn't have gotten to you in time so I called your brother to see where they were. I'm glad I did. There's no telling what that bitch had."

"You good sis?" Jax asked me.

"Yea. Haven can you follow me home?"

"You already know." Jax jumped in the car with Venus and it just so happened that they all followed me.

I opened the door and my grandmother went off and wanted to go back and fight the two bitches. Haven called her on the way and told her what happened.

After they all left, I hopped in the shower and laid down in my bed naked. I was tired and just wanted to go to sleep.

"Journey you have company." My grandmother said and opened the door. I hated that she never knocked but it's how she was.

When he walked in my grandmother had a smirk on her face like the shit was funny. I pulled the covers over my body and looked around the room for my robe. I saw it hanging up on the closet door across the room.

"Are you ok?" Colby asked and sat down next to me.

"Yea I'm fine." He examined my face and planted a kiss on my lips.

"I'm sorry she stepped to you. I'm gonna handle it."

"It's ok. She wanted to let me know you were her man I guess."

"About that. What you saw earlier…" I put my hand up.

"You don't have to explain. That's your girl and I'm just…"

"You're just what I need." He said cutting me off and pressing his lips on mine.

I lifted my arms around his neck exposing my chest because the cover fell. I tried to cover up, but he stopped me. I watched him go over and lock my bedroom door.

"I want you Journey." He took his shirt off and his body was perfectly cut in a V.

"I want you too but I've never…" He kissed me and laid my body down on the bed.

His kisses went from my lips, to my neck and then my

breast. He sucked on each one softly and my body was on fire. I had my hand on his head as he went back and forth pleasing both of them. His head moved down to my belly button where his tongue went in and out.

"You good ma?" I shook my head yes and covered my face as he put his mouth on my treasure. The feeling he gave me had my entire body shaking. Every lick, each time his fingers went in and out and the sucking had me release in his mouth three times.

"Your pussy is the best I ever tasted." He said when he came up to kiss me. His tongue danced with mine again and I felt his dick hardening up under me.

"We don't have to do this now. I can wait Journey." He said staring down at me.

"I want you to be my first Colby. I don't expect anything in return. This feeling right now you're giving me; I don't want it to end." He smiled and kissed me again. He removed the rest of his clothes and I felt the tip of him at my tunnel and got nervous.

"Baby it's going to hurt I'm not going to lie. But I

promise to make it feel good right after." He whispered in my ear. It took him a few minutes to enter and each try felt like he was trying to break open my pussy.

"Fuck Journey. I knew you were going to feel this good." He moaned out and gave me slow strokes. The pain eventually turned to pleasure and I was having my first orgasm through penetration. I've always heard women say they couldn't get one that way, but Colby did it and the feeling was even better than when I had those few orally.

"Colby it feels so good. Please don't stop."

"Journey I don't know what we're doing but I'm not going to be able to leave you alone." He pushed my legs to my shoulders and had me grabbing the headboard. The way I was moaning I know damn well my grandmother heard me.

"Do you wanna try and ride me?" I shook my head yes even though I was nervous.

"Are you going to teach me what to do?" He said yes and let out a moan as I slid down.

Don't laugh at me."

"Never baby." He moved my hips the way he wanted

102

me until I caught the rhythm. He smacked my ass a few times, which turned me on more and made me cum all over him. I stood up on my feet and went up and down.

"Ahhh shit Journey. I'm about to cum."

"You are?" I was excited I was able to please him enough to cum. He sat up and looked down at my pussy to watch himself go in and out of me.

"Fuckkkkk." He yelled out and held my body tight.

"Damn Journey. This pussy right here is dangerous." He said after we came together. He had me lying on his chest still trying to catch my breath. I lifted my head and moved closer to kiss him.

"Can I go down on you?" He sat up on his elbows looking as shocked as I was saying it.

"Nah. You not ready for that."

"Who says?"

"Have you ever given head?"

"No. But it can't be that hard."

"We can wait Journey." He said and I started kissing on his chest and working my way down. I felt him getting aroused.

"You're just going to do what you want."

"Yup. If you're going to be my first, then I may as well try everything with you." He grabbed my hand and led me in the bathroom. He asked me where the towels were and turned the shower on.

"Why are we getting in the shower?"

"Because this was your first time, which means there's blood on both of us. I'm not going to let you give me head like that." Then I remembered we didn't use protection. I can't get pregnant the first time anyway. *Can I?* The thought left my mind as he took his time washing my body. When he got in between my legs it was sore, but he was gentle. The water was rinsing off the soap as we kissed, and I stroke him until he was hard.

"You sure Journey." I didn't answer and licked the tip before placing him in my mouth. He was pretty big and thick but like most women I've watched enough porn to know I have to pace myself.

"Yea Journey." He said quietly but I heard him. I jerked him off, made my way down to his balls and sucked on each one.

"Yoooo." He grabbed on to the walls.

"Am I supposed to swallow?" I asked before I put him back in my mouth.

"You don't have to." He said. I bobbed my head faster and used my hand to play with his balls.

"Journey you sucking the hell out of my dick. Fuck baby." He moaned out and grabbed the back of my hair.

"I'm cumming Journey you can get up." I stayed in position and when I felt something hitting my throat, I suctioned my cheeks in and sucked until I felt him go soft.

I glanced up at him and his head was facing the ceiling. It was like he didn't want to look at me and that shit had me feeling some kind of way. I went to step out the shower and he grabbed me back in.

"That was the best head I ever got." He started kissing me and before I knew it, he had me bent over in the shower screaming out his name.

"Colby, I'm cumming again."

"Me too."

"Sssss." I felt my juices leave my body and tried to move but couldn't. He gave me another quick wash up and sat me on the chaise at the end of my bed.

"Where are your clean sheets?" I pointed to the linen closet in the bathroom. I saw him change the sheets and place the other ones in the hamper. He lifted me up and put me in the bed. I noticed him check his phone, type something in and seconds later he was right behind me.

"Journey."

"It's ok Colby. I'm not expecting anything from you. I wanted this and you. I just want to go to sleep."

"Journey." He tried to talk again, and I refused to hear him say that we couldn't be together.

"Colby, just give me this moment. I know you have other obligations, just let me have these last moments with you." He blew his breath out and didn't say anything. I don't know when I fell asleep nor do I remember him leaving. But I guess after getting dicked down like that I wouldn't.

****

The next morning, I woke up tired as hell. I picked my

phone up to check the time and it was twelve in the afternoon. I was glad it was Saturday and didn't have classes.

I made myself get out of bed and almost fell. My legs were weak as hell and my pussy was sore. The crazy part is that sore or not I wanted more.

I went to the bathroom and got straight in the shower. I brushed my teeth, washed my face and went to find some sweats to throw on.

"He put that ass to sleep last night huh?" My grandmother said cracking up when I stepped in the kitchen.

"Must you speak like that so early in the morning?"

"Child please. It's already the afternoon. And did you know he just left an hour ago?"

"He did?"

"Yup. He wanted me to tell you he was going to a funeral and he wanted to see you later. He left his number." She passed it to me, and I quickly put it in my phone. I wasn't to going to use it today but I was definitely using it.

Wolf

I was mad as hell when Jax got the call that some bitches were trying to fuck with my sister. Journey wasn't a fighter, but we taught her how to. The only thing she never wanted to happen to her was being beat on by multiple people, which possibly could've happened if we didn't show up.

I knocked the hell out of that other girl and gave zero fucks afterwards. My parents may not have been able to raise me that long, but they taught me better than that.

Today was the chicks' funeral I murked at the club last week and to show respect I thought it was only right to show up. I mean I was the last face she saw before she took her last breath.

Jax and I both had on all black but not funeral attire. We were in hoodies and jeans with black Timbs. We looked damn good if I must say so myself. The reason behind us going was to see if this *Freedom* dude would show his face. It's not like we knew what he looked like but with us showing up he's bound to see us.

"Damn did she have any friends?" I asked walking in and taking a seat in the back row. There weren't many people here, but I did see this other bitch I fucked sitting in the front row.

"Yo is that Venus with her head on some dudes shoulder?" I asked Jax who was ready to blow a gasket. I guess she hadn't told him she was going.

"Yea that's her and some nigga named Colby. I swear I'm killing both of them if I find out their fucking."

"Colby" I haven't seen him in about a year. Let me say what's up?" I went to stand but Jax had me sit down since the service was starting.

A few more people came in and I noticed Venus turn around when an older guy sat behind them. He leaned in and said something that made her get up and move to another seat. Jax and I shrugged our shoulders but continued watching.

"Baby, what are you doing here?" Venus asked Jax when the funeral was over. It wasn't long and it seemed like everyone was ready to go.

"The question is, what are you doing here and who's the nigga you had your head resting on? Venus don't make me kill your ass."

"Whatever. That's Colby."

"What's up Colby?" I said when he came over to us. Jax was ice grilling the fuck out of him. When Venus introduced him as her brother, I laughed hard as hell at my Jax.

"What's so funny?" Venus asked me.

"Your man here was ready to kill both of y'all if you two were fucking."

"Damn Venus what you do to him that has him ready to kill for you?"

"I got that good, good don't I baby?" She kissed Jax and he pulled her closer.

"Ok y'all just had to be extra." I told them and gave Colby a man hug.

"What y'all doing here?" I was about to answer him when the chick I used to fuck with came to where we were.

"I'm ready Colby." She said. I stood there with my arms folded staring at her to see if she would speak.

"Ok. I'll be ready in a few minutes. Go to the car." She rolled her eyes and did what he said.

"You know my girl?"

110

"Your girl. How long have you been with her?" I asked but not really wanting to know the answer.

"A few years."

"Word On some real shit you need to dump her."

"Why is that?"

"Yo I've been fucking her for the last year. I just stopped a few months ago. Her name is Whitney or some shit like that."

"Willow." Colby responded with a laugh.

"My bad yo. I ain't know she was taken."

"It's all good. I was breaking up with her after the funeral and this is just the ammunition I need."

"Damn that's cold."

"Nah, we were having issues for a while and I met someone. She's already made me fall for her. This woman got in my head and now I don't see anyone but her."

"She must have whatever your sister has. How both of y'all strung out?"

"It's not even about the sex with this one. She's different from these bitches out here and it's what drew me too

111

her. She's classy as hell and her being around makes me want to slow down."

"Wow. She does all that bro?" Venus asked him like she knew who he was talking about.

"All that and a whole lot more. I'll see you guys later." He kissed his sister and dipped off.

"Oh my boy Derrick just proposed to his girl and we'll be at Club Jax. You should come hang out."

"Not Derrick Madison." Jax yelled out.

"Yup that's him." Colby was walking backwards.

"We'll be there." I yelled to him as he got in the car.

"You ready to go?" Jax asked Venus.

"Yea. I only came because my brother didn't want to come by himself." We hopped in my truck and went to check on Journey. I parked in front of the house and she opened the door to greet us. I snatched her ass up quick as hell with Jax on my heels.

"Who the fuck is he?"

"What are you talking about and get off me?"

"Journey did you lose your virginity?" Jax asked and

112

she looked over to Venus who was just as shocked.

"I'm grown. Why are you questioning me anyway?"

"Journey you just told us you didn't have a man and you were still pure. You open the door with not one but two damn hickeys on your neck. That only means one thing." I said grabbing a glass and pouring myself a shot.

"Once again I'm…"

"Journey I don't give a fuck if you were thirty-five, I'm still going to question you. Who is this nigga and where does he live?" I asked and Jax followed up with his own threat.

"Does he know your brothers are gonna kill him?"

"Now wait a minute guys." Venus jumped in and we both looked at her like she had two heads.

"I'm just saying, we all know how smart your sister is and I'm sure whoever she was with and if she did lose it, it's with someone she cares deeply about. You two know she is not like that."

"What the hell is going on out here?" Grams said and came out with just a robe on. The girls started laughing.

"Grams what were you doing?" I asked and stared at

113

her tryna cover herself up.

"I was fucking until I heard all this racket out here."

"Yo! Grams don't ever say that shit again." Jax was mad as hell.

"Grams your granddaughter has given herself away." I told her.

"And."

"And." Both of us said at the same time.

"And she doesn't have a man. At least not one we've checked out and she's giving away her stuff." I couldn't even say the word I was so disappointed in her.

"Well I met the man twice and I must say your sister has some good taste. And by the way he had her screaming, I would say he did a damn good job at breaking her in." All our mouths hit the floor when she said that. Journey hit the ground like she passed out, but she was laughing so hard she fell over the chair.

"Shoot, the shit had me ready to fuck but my man wasn't here, so I had to make it up tonight."

"Stop playing Grams." Jax said walking to help

Journey up.

"Listen, your sister knows how much you love her, and you know she isn't a dummy. If she gave someone her virginity it's because she has feelings for him, and it was what she wanted. You have to remember she is older than you, yet; you two nasty dogs have been fucking since you were twelve. You need to be giving her credit for waiting as long as she did. Now take your asses home so I can finish riding…"

"Grams I'm out." Jax said snatching Venus hand and walking out the front door. I don't know where the hell he was going when I'm the one who drove him over here.

I gave Journey a hug and told her I was sorry for snapping on her. I wish she would've waited so I could've checked the nigga out or something. I told her to lock up and went to take these other two to Jax house.

"What up Journey?" I spoke in my phone when she called.

"I'm putting an ad in the paper for a bookkeeper. I've been really busy with school work and student teaching." I blew my breath out. Journey knew we didn't want anyone but family in our business.

"Why didn't you just ask Grams to do it? I can pick the books up every week and bring them to her."

"Fine. Tell Grams I'll pay her, and she starts next Friday."

"Thanks Haven."

"Yea. Yea." I made sure to stop at every red light because the cops were out tonight.

"Haven."

"What Journey?"

"I love you bro."

"I love you too sis."

"Is Jax still in the truck." She asked.

"Yup but he's in the back finger fucking Venus."

"No he's not Journey. Really Wolf."

"I love you Jax."

"I love you too sis."

I hung the phone up and told Jax I would be back to pick him up to go by the club later. Venus didn't seem too pleased but that wasn't my problem.

I went to Wal-Mart to grab a few things for my house. I had about ten items in my hand so I stood in the express line. I don't care what anyone says this store has to be the most ratchet and unprofessional workplace in the world. How every cashier ringing shit up always have an attitude?

It was my turn for the cashier to ring me up but I saw her close out her register and another chick came behind her and put her register in. This chick was actually pretty when she smiled. She was brown skinned with a decent looking shape. Her face reminded me of that Dej Loaf girl. She had an earring in her lip, and I saw one in her eyebrow.

"How are you today sir?" She said sliding my items across the scanner.

"I'm good. How are you Passion?" I asked reading her nametag. She smiled and finished ringing me up.

"That will be twenty-four fifty-five sir."

"Wolf. Wolf is my name."

"Wolf. Like an animal."

"Just like the animal baby." I handed her a fifty and waited for my change. I could've told her to keep it but I didn't want her to lose her job because she was pocketing the change.

"What's up with your number?" I asked and stepped to the side.

"I don't have one."

"What the fuck? Who doesn't have a cell phone? Shorty, if you don't want to give it out just say it." She smiled and continued ringing up the people.

"I don't have one is all I'm going to say. I don't know you to be discussing my business."

"Her man kicked her and their son out and he wouldn't let her take anything." Some chick came up behind me telling her business.

"Darlene stop telling my business."

"Girl this nigga fine as hell. You better stop playing the shy role and get with him." The chick Darlene said and went back to her register.

"Word. The nigga on some fuck shit like that?" I saw the way the other customers were looking at me but I didn't care.

I walked to the back of the store where the electronics

department was and asked to see some cell phones. I got her one of those prepaid ones and had the dude add minutes to it. I paid and he handed me the phone with the receipt to it.

"Here shorty." She was standing there talking because there were no customers in line.

"I can't take this from you." She pushed the phone in my hand.

"Yes, you can. I put my number in it. You should always have a phone if you have a kid anyway; anything could happen. When I call make sure you answer?"

"Oh she will." The other chick yelled out. I walked back to her when I noticed she had a tear coming down her face.

"Yo, come here." I pulled her to the side.

"Look, I've never done shit for anyone before if they weren't family. The reason I'm saying this is because you look like you're in a bad situation and need help." She didn't say anything and let more tears fall.

"Stop crying. Do you have anywhere to stay?"

"No she doesn't. She's staying with me but it is pretty

tight."

"Yo, do you ever mind your business? I mean you barely let her speak."

"My sister is my business and I speak for her because she won't. That nigga fucked her up so bad mentally, when a man tries to be nice to her this is what she does and then he backs off." She stepped away from her register.

"Listen, I know you think I'm being nosy but I'm just looking out for my sister. It may be tight at my house, but she will always have some place to go you can be sure of that." She said and went back to her register to ring up customers.

"What time do you get off?"

"Ten. Why?" She wiped her tears.

"That's in two hours. I'll be here to pick you up."

"I don't know you like that."

"You're right so I'm going to bring my sister with me. Trust me she's not going to allow me to bring any harm to you." She agreed and I found myself watching her walk back to the register. I don't know what man did her wrong but to throw her out with her son is some real fuck nigga shit.

I was supposed to be on my way home to get dressed but I sent a message to Journey to meet me at my condo I used when I didn't feel like driving home and told Jax to come with Venus. I parked in my spot and walked inside. It smelled like old garbage when I opened the door.

"What the hell Haven? I told you I was busy with school work." Journey said when she came in ten minutes later.

"What up bro and why does it smell like that in here?"

"Yuk Wolf. Whoever she is needs to die." Venus sassed.

"Ha ha, very funny y'all. I need you three to help me clean up. I'm about to move someone in here." They all snapped their heads back. Journey came over to feel my forehead and Jax started laughing. I saw Venus give a crazy look too.

"Listen don't laugh when I tell you the story either." I explained to them everything that went down, and the two girls jumped up and hugged me.

"What's that for?"

"Because you're finally bringing someone here who

isn't a jump-off. Do you think you'll make her your main chick?" Journey said as she and Venus started cleaning up the place.

"Damn y'all I was just giving her a place to stay. I can't have her and her son out there in the streets like that."

"Righhhhtttt." They both said at the same time.

"Venus, I'm going to need you to hook her up at the salon and sis I'm going to give you some money to take her and the kid shopping tomorrow."

"You're doing a lot for someone you just met." Jax said and I agreed but something in me told me to do it.

After we cleaned the house Journey jumped in the car with me and my brother and his girl went to his house. Venus said she would meet her tomorrow and Jax said he'll see her whenever.

****

"Just go please." I heard Passion saying as I walked up on her and some dusty ass dude from the neighborhood I knew.

"Hell no bitch. You got my son."

"You kicked me and your son out for that Willow bitch

who doesn't even want you. That bitch has a rich boyfriend. I was the one that stayed there for you and this is how you treat me? Just leave me alone." *Willow is a hoe like that?* I thought to myself.

"What's the problem my man?" I asked and all the blood drained from his face when he saw me.

"Nothing Wolf. Me and my girl were just discussing some things."

"Nah, I think I heard her tell you to leave her alone." I looked at her and she nodded her head yes.

"Come on man. I don't want any problems but…"

"Yo, is this the nigga that kicked you and your son out?"

"Yes."

"Go wait in the car." I told dude to take a walk with me around the building.

"Listen here. Whatever you had going on with her is over. If you want to see your son contact me since you took her cell phone. I better not hear you disrespected her or you're out here talking bad about her. Do I make myself clear?"

"Wolf, come on." I dug my hand in my pocket and pulled out two pills.

"Swallow these fucking pills." He was shaking his head no.

I put my gun under his chin, he opened up real quick and tossed the pills in his mouth. I stood there for two minutes when his body went into convulsions and he hit the ground. His eyes started rolling and you could see his body shutting down on him.

"Wolf come on." I heard Journey yell. She knew not to call me by my real name in public.

Once I saw him laid out on the ground, I put a call in to my peoples to have him picked up and left. I didn't have to introduce the girls because they were talking when I got in the car. She asked me to stop by her sisters to pick up her son and get some clothes for them. We waited for about ten minutes when she came out with two suitcases I put in the trunk. She ran back in and came out with her son. He couldn't have even been one yet by how small he was.

"How old is he?" Journey asked looking back there.

"Seven months."

"He is very handsome. I can't wait to meet him when he's awake." We got to the condo and I carried her son in and left the suitcases in the trunk. She walked in and started crying right away.

"Are you ok?" Journey was rubbing her back.

"Yea. I'm just not used to someone being nice to me." I heard her say and went upstairs to put the baby in the bed. I brought all her stuff in and told her where everything was.

I walked my sister outside and she instantly felt bad for her. She and I talked for about ten minutes and I gave her a hug goodbye. I went inside to say goodbye to Passion, and she was coming out the shower with a towel wrapped around her. The way the towel clung to her body had my dick brick hard.

"My bad. I just wanted to tell you I was leaving."

"Thank you Wolf and just let me know when we have to leave."

"Leave. You can stay here as long as you want."

"I can?"

"Yes. I don't come here so you can call this place yours

125

just don't be having a bunch of people here. The white people don't play that." I told her laughing.

She let her towel fall and I'll be damned if her body wasn't flawless. All I wanted to do was throw her ass on the bed and fuck the shit out of her, but I couldn't. I picked the towel up and wrapped it around her.

"Shorty, I did this because I wanted to. Not because I expected anything in return."

"Oh my goodness. Thank you because I've never been with any man besides my sons' father and I don't know you like that. I thought since you let me stay here I had to." I put my finger to her lips to stop her from speaking.

"If a man expects pussy from you just because he did something nice then he's not a man. Real men do it because they want to. Remember that." I kissed her cheek and walked out, locking the door behind me. I had to stay away from this condo because shorty was definitely going to make me put it on her.

Jax

"Suck that shit Venus." I grabbed the back of her hair and watched her digest all my cum. I lifted her up and made her get on the bed. I couldn't get enough of fucking her and she knew it.

I rubbed the tip on her pussy and my dick got hard instantly. I entered her from behind and pounded inside her. The smacking of her ass to my pelvis was all that could be heard.

"Jax baby don't stop. I'm cumming again. I love you. Shit, I love youuuuuuu." She came so hard my dick was almost fully white. A few minutes later I was right behind her. I waited until I let all my seeds run to find a hiding spot in her pussy. I wanted a baby and Venus was going to be the one to carry it. Did she know I wanted that no, but we've never used a condom and she never asked me to pull out?

"I love you too girl." Come take a shower with me." I grabbed her hand and we washed each other up. I wrapped her in a towel and walked out to find something to wear. She threw on one of my shirts since she was at my house and got in the bed.

I put on some dark blue denim Armani jeans with and Armani shirt to match. My sneakers were by Balenciaga and my jewelry was by Jacob the jeweler. I was shining bright tonight.

"Move in with me Venus." I whispered in her ear when she walked over to me and started kissing on my neck.

"Jax, don't you think it's too soon?"

"Venus, we've been kicking it well over a year and you've been my girl for the last few months. We're together all the time. What's the problem?"

"The problem is the bitches calling you on a cell phone you just got since you been out of jail. The only way they got your number is if you gave it to them." She just snapped out of nowhere with that. I wasn't cheating on her but the chicks from my job did have my phone number, but they were supposed to I was the boss.

"Venus, I told you I'm not cheating on you. Yes, I see women all the time there's no mistaken that but you're the only one I want. You have the code to my house, the keys to my crib, you know the passcode to my phone, and everyone knows you're my girl. I know Penny fucked your head up when she lied but Venus, I want you to carry my kids and one day be my wife."

"Really Jax." She wrapped her arms around my neck.

"Really Venus but you have to stop being insecure. If you want, I'll get my number changed and only the club manager will have it. You're right the strippers are to go to him first anyway and shouldn't have my number."

"I love you so much Jax and I just don't want to lose you. I'm scared that you were just jail talking me. My feelings are in too deep and I don't think I could take it if…"

"Stop right there Venus." I made her look at me.

"I'm not sticking my dick in any woman but you and I damn sure ain't giving my kids to anyone else. If I were a jail talking dude I would've fucked around already. We'll talk about this some more when I get home later." I told her when I heard my brother out there blowing.

"We don't have to and I'm going to leave it alone now. Have fun tonight."

"Good night Venus." I kissed her and went downstairs

to get in the car. I made sure the doors were locked and hopped in.

We pulled in the back of the club and since it was Saturday it was packed like always. I text the guard at the door and had him open it for me. The two of us walked straight into the VIP section and saw Colby, Derrick and a few other dudes in there. Drew came in a few minutes after us and joined the party. I had the waitress keeping everyone's glassed filled. I noticed Colby paying more attention to his phone then what was going on around him.

"Yo, what the hell you doing? I thought this was a party for your boy and you can't leave the phone alone." I said to him.

"Nah, it's my new shorty. She wants me to stop by when I'm done, and I can't leave her hanging."

"Well at least you're not with the other chick."

"Yea, I'm good on that." He and I finished talking for a while when I decided to go upstairs and call my girl. I left the door open and sat down listening to the phone ring.

This chick really had me open over her and to be honest

I loved it. The door shut and when I looked up it was one of the strippers that had been hitting on me. I never told Venus because she would've been up here quick.

"What can I do for you Blossom?" I didn't realize I had the phone in my ear. She came to where I was and sat on the edge of the desk.

"Listen, I know you just came home from jail and haven't been able to fuck because you're on lockdown, but I promise I won't tell."

"Blossom let's be clear on one thing. I'm not sure what type of niggas you've been around but my girl means everything to me. I'm not trying to destroy what we have on a piece of ass that everyone in this town most likely had. Second, my girls' pussy is so good I don't need another bitch. Now if you'll excuse me."

"She may have good pussy but it ain't mine." She said and moved in front of me with her legs cocked open. I can't front she had a pretty pussy and I could tell she was wet by the way it was glistening. She put her fingers inside, took one out and placed it in her mouth.

"Look, you got to go." My dick was brick hard, but I wasn't going to let her know.

"I think you want me to stay." She had her hand on my buckle just as the door opened. Venus stood there staring with hurt written on her face. Blossom jumped off my desk, put her clothes on and ran out the office. I thought for sure Venus would hit her but she didn't.

"It's not what it looks like baby. I swear."

"Jax, I came here tonight to say I was sorry for always bringing up that jail talk and accusing you of sleeping around." She opened her jacket and all she had on was a sheer teddy proving that she was there for that reason. I saw her close it and tie the belt tight on it.

"Venus baby, I'm telling you I didn't touch her."

"Really Jax because it didn't look like that and your dick is hard." I looked down and it was.

"Jax, I trusted and believed you, but I guess its true. You can do a one-year bid or a twenty-year bid with a nigga, he's still going to cheat on you when he comes home. Goodbye Jax." I jumped in front of her, shut the door and made sure I locked it. I unloosened the coat and ripped that teddy off her body. I unbuckled my jeans and let them fall with my boxers. I lifted her up and slid her down on my dick and fucked her against the wall.

"Jax, stop. I don't want to fuck you after you've been with someone else."

"Be quiet Venus and fuck me back." She bit down on my shoulder and popped up and down on me. We both came a few minutes later. I went in the bathroom and grabbed some paper towels to wipe her down. I came back and she was gone. I ran out the office to catch her but she was nowhere in sight. I asked the guard where she went, and he said she ran out the back door.

"Fuck." I went back upstairs and slammed the door to my office. I went downstairs and found that bitch Blossom dancing on Wolf and snatched her up.

"Everything ok boss?" She said like she didn't know what was going on.

"Bitch you're fired. Get your shit and get out. If I see you lurking around here, I'm going to slit your throat." I asked

Wolf for his keys and told Drew to make sure he got home.

I drove straight to Venus house and just like I thought her ass was in the shower. She didn't even know I came in. I sat on the edge of the bed waiting for her to come out.

"Go back to your hoe."

"You are my hoe." I pulled her arm and made her sit on my lap.

"If you ever run out the club naked like that again I'm gonna fuck you up."

"Whatever." She got down on her knees and gave me some head out of nowhere. She had me cumming in no time.

"What was that for? I thought you were mad at me." She picked her phone up and let me hear the conversation I had with Blossom. It was at that moment I remembered I never hung the phone up which was a good thing for me. I pulled her hair back and made her look in my eyes.

"I told you I wouldn't cheat on you and for the last time I'm not a jail talking nigga."

"I'm sorry."

"Say what?"

"I said I'm sorry."

"You better be. Now assume the position. I'm about to fuck the shit out of you some more until you learn your lesson."

"Come on Jax. You did a good job at the club."

"Nah, that's nothing compared to what I'm about to do to you." I dog fucked the hell out of her and when she fell asleep, I woke her up and did it again. I bet her ass wouldn't pull that leaving shit again.

✳✳✳✳✳✳✳✳✳✳✳

"Bitch why you walking funny and why aren't you ready?" I heard Journey say to Venus when I walked down the steps.

"Ask your brother. He was on some animalistic shit last night." She pointed to me.

"Ok never mind. I do not want to know what you two did."

"Hey sis. I was thinking." I said kissing her cheek.

"About?" She was sipping on a bottle of soda she just took out the fridge.

135

"About meeting the guy you're with. I have an idea of who it is but I don't want to say and it be wrong."

"You have an idea? How is that even possible? You don't see me with anyone and he and I aren't a couple."

"So why you fucking him?"

"Jax." Venus yelled out and I gave her a look.

"Fuck that look you're giving me. I'm tired of the way you and your brother come at her like she's some hoe."

"Venus you're overstepping."

"No I'm not. She may be your blood sister, but she is still mine as well. Stop talking to her like she's a kid." She wrapped her arms around my waist.

"Baby, she can make her own decisions and all she needs from you and your brother is to trust her in making the right choices. The guy she is with must be doing something right because I haven't seen her this happy in a long time." I looked at Venus and smiled.

"Are you happy sis?"

"I'm happy having fun Jax. I'm not expecting anything from him. He just got out of a relationship and I'm not trying to pressure him into another one. And just so you know, I think

you would like him." I didn't say anything, grabbed something

to eat and took my ass back upstairs to lie down. Venus may

have shit to do but I didn't, and a nigga was going back to

sleep as soon as she left.

"Don't think because you stood up to me for my sister,

I won't fuck you up."

"Jax, I know you three have a bond and I'm not trying

to break it. But you also have to remember she isn't as tough as

the two of you mentally. The way you say things to her seem

harsh and whether you know it or not you hurt her feelings.

She's not a hoe and she really likes this guy. She wants you to

meet him but she doesn't want you to scare him away. Baby let

her have fun. It's been a long time and she deserves it." She

kissed my lips and got up to leave.

"You know who it is." I wanted to see what she would

say.

"My lips are sealed. She will tell you soon enough."

And with that she walked out, and I took my ass back to sleep.

Colby

The night Journey let me make love to her, I wanted to tell her the real reason why I was interested in her at the beginning. I didn't want any secrets that I knew would eventually come out. Unfortunately, she wouldn't allow me to and ever since I've just been avoiding it altogether.

The moment I entered her, I knew she was going to be mine and I had to protect her from whatever the hell my father had going on. I called up my brother Wesley and told him to meet me at my dad's to see if he would tell us. When he didn't, I told him the deal was off with Journey and walked out. That was the same day as the funeral. He had the nerve to come up in there saying that if I didn't go through with the plan, he would hurt Venus. I was about to turn around and say something, but the service started.

Willow was a mess but more so because Journey fucked her up good. She had to get five stitches in her head, her lip was busted, and she had some bruises on her face she had to cover with makeup.

"So you're going to sit in my car and act like you didn't fuck that nigga." It was the day after the funeral and I wanted to break shit off. She stared out the window and I could see the tears coming down her face. I don't know if it was over her sister or me.

"Colby, I love you. Shit, I'm in love with you but you neglected me so much I turned to someone else. No, it wasn't right and I should've told you. But what did you expect me to do when you were never around?" I didn't know what to say because I thought she would deny it, but hearing her own up to it had me looking at her differently.

I did neglect her, but it was because of business not some other women. If she would've asked me, I had no problem telling her but she took it upon herself to be sneaky.

"Maybe this isn't what you want Willow and that's fine. We can still be cool." I felt her hand undoing the button on my jeans. I moved her hands away.

"No thanks Willow." She ignored me. I went to pull over to stop and by the time I did she already had me in her mouth. I grabbed on to the middle console and the door handle.

139

"Fuck Willow. I'm cumming."

"Mmmm." She moaned out and for some reason she swallowed everything I had in me. I stared at her when she lifted up. There was something different about her but I wasn't sure what it was. I buttoned my pants up and dropped her off at home.

I drove to my house in deep thought about what just happened. I took a shower to get ready for the party, left my house around eleven and found Derrick and some of our other boys sitting in VIP when I got there. The drinks were coming back to back thanks to Jax. A text came through on my phone from and unknown number.

Unknown: *Thanks for last night. Can I see you tonight?"* I smiled when I read her text. This was the first phone conversation we had since we've known one another. Neither of us exchanged numbers so I left mine with her grandmother.

Me: *Are you sure you can hang? I mean last night was your first time you should be sore."*

My Journey: *You don't worry about all that. Just*

make sure you please my entire body again."

Me*: I'm on my way."* She didn't respond after that. I looked at the time and it was a little after one in the morning. I dapped everyone up and told them I would speak to them tomorrow.

The entire ride over to her house all I thought about was making love to her. I loved the way she screamed my name out and the best part is knowing I'm the only one who touched her. I walked up to the door, sent her a text telling her I was outside, and she shocked the hell out of me when she opened it.

"I would've come over a long time ago if I knew you were waiting for me like this." She had a satin robe on with a pair of black lace panties, no top and some red bottom shoes on.

"I wanted you to have fun first."

"Nah, shorty this is way better." I lifted her up kissing her and shut the door with my foot. I carried her upstairs to her room and laid her down gently on the bed.

"You are so fucking beautiful Journey and you're all mine." I removed the panties and kept her shoes on.

141

I lifted her leg, licking and sucking all over her and found my new favorite place waiting to be touched. Her pearl was already rock hard, and her juices were seeping out slowly. I slid my tongue up and down and watched her arched her back.

"Colby make me cum baby." Her moaning was doing something to me. I told her to get on all fours.

"What are you doing?"

"I'm about to make that pussy cum just like you asked." I took my shirt off and got behind her. I licked her ass and she jumped forward. I pulled her back, held her body and licked, sucked and made her cum so many times she fell on the bed.

"I'm feeling inside my pussy tonight Journey." I lifted her back up and turned her on her back. I pushed myself in and made love to her again. The way she bit her lip and threw her head back when she came made me go harder. The pleasure took over and her facial expressions would now be embedded in my head.

"Get on top." We switched positions and I let her go for a ride alone. I didn't have to guide her or anything. My baby was a fast learner and made me cum not too long after. For the next two hours we sexed each other down over and over.

She had just fallen asleep after we took a shower when I heard my phone going off non-stop. I picked it up and it was Willow begging me to stay the night with her. I didn't have to think about that shit, turned my phone off and laid under my new woman with no regrets. She took my hand and laid it across her chest.

"She wants you back. If that's what you want to do, then be gone by the time I wake up in the morning." She told me. I guess she wasn't asleep after all.

"I don't want her. I only want you Journey."

"Are you sure? You just broke up with her."

"Positive."

"Can I tell people about us?"

"As long as it's not your grandmother. I think she wants me." She elbowed me in the stomach. She and I fell asleep right after that and I stayed with her until the next afternoon.

I really didn't have a choice because it's when I woke

143

up. I felt someone stroking my dick and opened my eyes just as Journey was about to put it in her mouth. I could never get enough of this. She wasn't lying when she said she would cater to her man as much as he did to her.

Once we sexed one another for another hour I told her it was time for me to leave and I would call her later. I found myself wanting to lay up with her all day, but I never officially broke it off with Willow. We haven't really been together as a couple, but we still held the title. After she sucked my dick the day after the funeral, I dropped her off and haven't spoken to her since.

I took a shower, changed my clothes and went by her house to get the shit over with.

"What's up Willow?" I asked when she opened the door. She stepped aside to allow me access inside. I walked over to sit on the couch, but something told me to turn around and when I did, I wish I didn't. Willow was ass naked, sitting on the chair with her legs wide open.

"I didn't come over here for this." I stood up to leave. I sexed my woman all night and I was tired. I wasn't about to cheat on her even though I hadn't broken up with Willow yet. I glanced down at my phone going off and smiled.

My Journey: *I miss you already. Have a good day*!

Me: *Same here and it's going to be a great day because I woke up next to the most beautiful woman in the world.*

My Journey: *You don't have to butter me up you got the* pussy.

Me: *I got you too.*

My Journey: *You sure do.* She sent me the emoji bowing me a kiss.

"I guess she got your head gone."

"What are you talking about?" I asked putting my phone back on the clip. She stood in front of me and started rubbing on my dick. I moved her hands out the way stepped back.

"I see you wanna play games. I'm just here to tell you it's over in person."

"It's not over. You're having fun with the new bitch, got some new pussy and you think you like her."

"Don't call her a bitch and as far as her being new

pussy and me liking her, you have no idea. She is my woman now and if I hear or even think you're disrespecting her in any way I'm coming for you."

"Damn she got you like that already?"

"Yup. Now put some clothes on." I told her and had my hand on the doorknob to leave until she said something that made me stop. I turned around and she had her hand on her hip like the shit was funny.

"What did you say?" She started picking something under her nails that probably wasn't there.

"How do you think she would take it if I told her your father made you pursue her? Or she's part of a plan that may get her killed?"

"Who told you that?'

"A little birdie. And the funny part is you don't even know why your pops have you doing it. But when you find out you're going to be mad you fell for the enemy's sister."

"I'm not with the enemy's sister. I don't even know her brothers."

"For now."

"Whatever. Just stay away from her."

"Maybe. Or maybe I'll go down to the college and tell her myself." I wanted to wring her fucking neck.

"What do you want Willow?"

"'Just you."

"I don't want you. Pick something else. You want money?"

"Nope. Just you." She said and pushed me back against the door. I didn't fight her this time when she pulled my man out and sucked me off until I came. This time she didn't swallow. She tried to kiss me but I turned my head.

"I want to fuck Colby."

"Nah I gave you some dick."

"Boy cut it out. I want to feel you inside me." I ran my hand down my face. I told her I would be right back and grabbed a few condoms out my car. If I had to do this to keep her mouth shut, I was strapping up. She was a hoe and I wasn't catching anything.

I came back in the house and she called me up to the bedroom. I made sure the front door was locked and went to her room. She was playing with her pussy. I removed my clothes, put on the condom and slid inside. She felt nothing like Journey nor were her moaning or facial expressions turning me on.

"Awww shit Colby. Fuck me harder. I'm about to cum." She yelled out and I did just that. She started screaming and the minute she scratched my back I knew I was fucked. Journey was bound to notice since she always told me my back was smooth and perfect. She didn't want to mess it up by scratching it. She would scratch my arms or grip the sheets tighter instead.

I pulled out, came in the condom and got up. I flushed it down the toilet and washed my hands. I looked in the mirror and felt like shit.

"Where are you going?" She asked when I started putting my clothes on.

"I do have other shit to do."

"I want to see you tonight."

"Not gonna happen." I told her because I meant that shit.

"Hmmmm. I think it will." She said and walked in the bathroom. I ran downstairs and grabbed my keys to leave.

I had to find a way to tell Journey before anyone else does. There's no way I can keep fucking Willow knowing at any time she can run to Journey with that information.

I called my brother up and told him I was on my way over. I walked in his house and he was playing the video game smoking. I picked up the other remote and had him start over.

"What's up nigga?"

"Man, I'm stuck between a rock and a hard place." He gave me a look to explain. I sat there telling him everything.

"How the fuck does she know? Wait, you think she fucking pops too?"

"I have no idea and at this point I don't really care. I just can't have her telling Journey. I'm telling you she'll never forgive my ass. She is fragile when it comes to people hurting her."

"Let me find out you really like her."

"I think I'm past the liking phase with her."

"It hasn't been that long for you to be in love."

"No but you can't help who you fall for and I'm not worried about how fast I fell. I think she feels the same."

"You want me to kill Willow? You know I have no problem with that. I can't stand her ass anyway."

"Nah I'm just going to have to figure this shit out."

"I suggest you tell Journey before Willow does. No woman you're supposed to be with wants to be the last to know."

"What about me fucking her?" I asked if I should mention it.

"Awww man deny that shit." I nodded my head and stayed a little while longer. I took my ass home and tried to come up with a way to tell Journey what was going on.

Journey

These last two months have been perfect between Colby and I. The day he took my virginity I couldn't get enough of him. The first day I was sore, but I took three baths that day and even though I was hurting, I wanted to feel him again. I sent him a text to come over and we've been a couple ever since.

We just came back from a week in Aspen he took me on for vacation. I still hadn't told my brothers about him yet. Not because I didn't want to but because they had their own things going on.

Venus just announced she was pregnant, and I was so happy to be an aunty. I was already planning the baby shower and Jax told me he was going to propose to her there. I was extremely happy for the two of them.

Wolf was in his own world right now with the Passion chick. I think he was falling for her and didn't know how to handle it. My brother has never been with just one woman. He hasn't told us she's his girl but his actions showed different.

Today, I had a doctor's appointment because I had been really sick this last week. Colby said it was because I ate that food from the seafood restaurant we tried out the other day. I checked in and noticed Colby's ex was working there.

Me: *I'm not in the mood for your ex. I'm going to whoop her ass if she gets out of line.*

My Baby: *Where are you?*

Me: *Doctors office*

My Baby: *I forgot to tell you she just started working there about a month ago.*

Me: *How the hell do you know?* I was curious to find out. He told me he hadn't seen or spoken to her since he told her it was over.

My baby: *I told you my brother goes to the same medical doctor. When he was sick last week, he told me he saw her there.* I wasn't sure if I believed him but he hasn't given me a reason to doubt his words either. I sat down in the waiting room and picked up a food magazine.

"Ms. Banks you can come back now." The nurse said. I followed behind her and noticed Willow roll her eyes. I ignored her because she was being childish. The nurse took my

vitals and said the doctor would be in shortly.

"Good morning Ms. Banks. What brings you in today?"

I explained to her the throwing up and dizzy spells.

"Is there a possibility you're pregnant?"

"I don't think so. My period just went off two weeks

ago." I told her.

"Ok. It could be food poisoning but to rule out

pregnancy I'm going to need a urine sample and blood work.

Also, you do know that you can still get your period and be

pregnant?"

"I've heard but isn't it rare?"

"It's not as rare as you think but yes it does happen."

She passed me the cup and had me go in the bathroom.

I came out after I finished, and she sent the nurse who

just walked in go and check it. The nurse called the doctor in

the bathroom and she told the nurse to go get some machine

and bring it back in.

"Ms. Banks the dizziness and vomiting is because you

are pregnant?" My mouth fell open and I started feeling dizzy again. She offered me some water and then told me to lay back on the bed.

"Are you ok?" I nodded my head yes when I should've said no. I wasn't ready for a kid. Hell, I was supposed to start a new job and I was still student teaching at the college.

Colby was good to me but would he be a great father? Did he even want kids? What was I thinking not making him wear a condom? I had so many thoughts going through my head I didn't even hear the doctor until she snapped her fingers.

"Are you sure you're ok?" She asked me. I told her yes and she had me stand up and told me to take everything off from the waist down and come back out. I was so nervous I almost fell when I tried to get back on the table. She pulled those stirrup things out and made me scoot down to the bottom.

"Ugh, this is a medical doctors office; what are you doing with a table like this in here?" I asked unsure of what was going on.

"Ms. Banks this is urgent care and we are here to take care of all needs, not just sickly people. We have multiple doctors here for different things."

"You can do that?"

"Yes and my medical coat says OB/GYN." I put my head down in embarrassment.

"But why didn't they send a medical doctor in?"

"Because once you gave the symptoms, they knew most likely it was a woman who was pregnant. Had the test come back negative then a different doctor would have come in." She inserted this fake dildo-looking thing and turned the screen to me.

"Ms. Banks have you been getting your period for the last few months?"

"Yes. I don't understand how I could be pregnant?"

"Well you are and you're three months." I started crying when she told me.

That means he got me pregnant when he broke my virginity. How stupid could I be? My brothers are going to kill him and me and they haven't even met him yet. She turned the screen to me, and I saw a tiny fetus inside me. I covered my face and laid there.

"I'm going to give you a minute to get yourself

155

together." She pulled the thing out and told me I could get dressed. When she closed the door, I put my clothes back on and picked up a paper towel to wipe the gel out of my vagina the best I could.

"Ms. Banks there are other options if this is not what you want." The doctor walked back in saying and handed me two photos of the baby I was carrying. My mom would roll over in her grave if I terminated this pregnancy. I informed the doctor I was just overwhelmed but there's no way I would get rid of it.

She handed me a prescription for vitamins and had me go out to the desk to set up a one-month appointment.

"Um doctor, I'm not comfortable with the person working the desk. Can you have the nurse who's been in here already set up the appointment and call me?"

"To be honest, I don't like her either. I hired her as a favor for my friend. Trust me she won't be here long, and I will have the nurse call you. Is this the correct number on file?" I nodded yes. She shook my hand and told me she would see me in four weeks.

I opened the door to the reception area, and it felt like all eyes were on me but they weren't.

"Well, well, well. Looks like somebody done knocked you up." I didn't have to turn around to know who it was but I did just so she didn't try and run up on me.

"What is it you want Willow? I don't fuck with you, but you always find a reason to fuck with me."

"I just want you to leave my man alone."

"If you're talking about Colby, he's my man."

"That's what you think." Something told me to get in my truck but the way she said it had me wondering what she meant by it.

"What is that supposed to mean?"

"It means just what I said. You think he's your man but he's not."

"Whatever." I tried to walk away, and she followed talking shit.

"I know all about your little Aspen trip you just came back from two days ago. But I bet you don't know where he was that night. Do you?" I thought about what she said and the night we came back he didn't stay because he claimed to have something to do.

"Ok. Why did he come to see you? Is that what you're getting at?"

"Oh he did more than come to see me."

"I doubt it." She laughed like what I said was funny.

"You think you have him strung out because you were a virgin when he fucked you but honey, he knows where home is. And the nights he's not with you I can guarantee he's with me." I can't believe he told her I was a virgin or better yet, he's been with her. It must be at night because we're always together.

"He told you I was a virgin?"

"No but if he's acting that way, I could guess that's why."

"Whatever. You'll say anything to make me leave him alone." I didn't want her to know she was getting to me.

"Look Journey. You seem like a nice person and I know you think I'm being a bitch but Colby isn't the man he says he is."

"You would say anything to hurt me."

"I admit in the beginning I didn't like you but he's lying to you and its best that you leave him alone before you get hurt worse."

"Why would I believe you?"

"I thought you would say that." She pulled her phone out and showed me text messages between the two of them. Some read that she wanted him to come over and he responded he was with me but if he got a minute he would stop by.

Others read she had a good time, but I also saw in one message him saying that he was going to tell me because he couldn't continue sleeping with her and holding it over his head. The messages went on and on and my nosy ass read each one for a good ten minutes until I got down to one that was a video.

"Don't you have to get back to work?" I passed her phone back to her.

"I'm on my fifteen-minute break. I have two minutes left. I see you haven't opened the video I sent him."

"For what? I don't want to see if you two are having

sex."

"No, I wouldn't want to either. But I do want you to hear what he said." She hit play and I didn't watch but I could hear the moaning going on between them.

"Do you still love me Colby?" At first you could hear the resistance in him.

"Colby do you still love me?"

"Ahhh Fuckkkkk Willow. Yes. Yes, I still love you. Shit girl. That was some of the best head I ever got." You could hear them kissing and that was it. I was done listening to the shit.

"Ok. What do you want now Willow?"

"Are you going to leave him alone?"

"Willow it could be old for all I know."

"Fine. If you don't believe me watch this." She sent a text to his phone asking him to come by in an hour for her lunch break and he responded with yes because he had plans tonight with me.

"How are you going to do that? You just took a break." I said trying not to believe the shit I just saw.

"I suddenly feel sick." The bitch yelled her address out on her way back in the doctors' office. I got in my car and drove off. I heard my phone going off and when I looked down it was Colby texting he was going to a meeting in an hour and I wouldn't be able to reach him. I tossed the phone on the seat and pulled over. I cried so hard I gave myself a headache. I didn't know what to do at this moment.

An hour later I parked down the street from the address Willow gave me and prayed Colby really had a meeting. Unfortunately, I saw him park in front of her house, get out, look around and went to the door. I called his phone and I could see him put his finger up to tell her to be quiet.

"Hey baby. You just caught me. I'm about to walk in my meeting right now."

"Oh ok. I guess I'll talk to you later."

"Wait! How did the doctor's appointment go?"

"She told me it was most likely food poisoning."

"I told you not to eat that nasty shit." I chuckled at how non-chalant he was and the fact that he was about to cheat on me. I told him to have fun at his meeting and that I would see

161

him later. I put my phone down and sat there to see how long he would be. Woman may say I'm crazy but I had to know. I don't know why but I did.

He came out about two hours later and had the nerve to give her a kiss as if they were a couple. He pulled off and my phone started ringing. I looked down and sent him to voicemail. If that nigga thought, he was going to play me. I had a trick for his ass.

I finally went home after seeing the bullshit and jumped in the shower. I still had the gel inside me regardless of wiping down with the paper towels. I wasn't sure how I would handle the situation string me in my face but it had to be dealt with.

I couldn't tell Venus because she would say something. My grandmother would definitely flip out because she loves him, and my brothers would probably kill him. This was going to be a one man's show I guess.

I was putting lotion on after I got out the shower when in walked Colby. He didn't have the same outfit on. At least he respected me that much to change. *Strike 1*. He tried to kiss me, but I turned my head due to the sight taking over my mind, I

162

witnessed earlier. *Strike 2*. He moved back and stared at me for a minute. The hickey on his neck was *Strike 3*.

"Colby. I don't think we're going to work out and I think it's best if we leave each other alone now before one of us ends up hurting the other." I wanted to say so much more but I wouldn't reveal anything yet.

"WHAT? You're breaking up with me."

"Yea. I was thinking with you all of sudden being busy and me student teaching and all we won't have the time for each other."

"Fuck that Journey. I can make time for you." He sat there looking at me with sad eyes.

"Colby, I haven't met anyone in your family but your sister and you have yet to meet my brothers. I just think that if either of us were serious about each other it would've happened already. And that brings me to believe that neither of us are ready for this relationship or whatever it is were doing." I stood up and my towel dropped. He grabbed me by the arm and pulled me closer to him. He knew how shy I was about seeing my body, but I wanted to see if he noticed anything different, and he didn't.

"Journey, I know things have changed since we first met but I promise it's not because of you. I have some things going on I can't discuss nor am I happy about doing."

"What is it?" I wanted to see if he would tell me. I could see him struggling to say it. I went to my drawer and took out some pajamas.

"And that's why we don't need to be together."

"Why?"

"I have been honest with you from day one. I never held any secrets from you, and I gave you something precious to me I can't get back. You're sitting here telling me you have things going on in your life but not telling me what it is so I can help you." He put his head in his hands.

"It's complicated Journey and I can't lose you."

"Colby, I can't be with someone who has secrets. Those secrets will eventually come out and whoever it has to do with is going to suffer the most because you held it from them. Just think about that." I opened the door for him.

"I'm not leaving Journey so you can stand there all

night." I didn't say anything and walked out the room.

"Grams can I sleep in here with you?" She was on her bed watching the news. She gave me a crazy look but patted the bed next to her.

"What's wrong Journey?"

"I thought Colby was the one but I guess I was wrong."

"What happened?"

"Things aren't always what they seem I guess."

"Did you tell him about the baby?" I looked over at her.

"How did you know?"

"Some nurse called the house phone to give me your appointment."

"Grams I just told him it was over and he doesn't want to leave. If I tell him, I'll never get rid of him. And what if he doesn't want kids?"

"If he didn't want them he wouldn't have trusted you with his sperm. Honey he knew what he was doing."

"You think he got me pregnant on purpose?"

"I'm not saying that but he's no fool either. You do know both of you will have to find a way to parent this child?"

I nodded my head and cuddled under her. She gets on my nerves but she's the closet person to a mother I have.

Venus

I was sitting in the living room labeling the boxes that were packed when I got a text from Journey telling me she was outside. I finally gave in to Jax and decided to move in with him. We found out last month I was eight weeks pregnant and he said I had to be living with him by the time the baby was born. He was happier then I was when the doctor told us. He was already looking online for baby furniture and clothes.

I opened the door for her, but I could see pain written on her face. I wasn't sure why because I spoke to her yesterday and she was fine. She told me she aced all her finals and wanted to celebrate.

I closed the door behind her and watched her go in one of the extra bedrooms I had. I figured she was tired, so I left her alone and finished what I was doing. She came out about an hour later.

"Hey you want to go to Red Lobster with me? I'm hungry." Journey asked and sat on the couch.

"Sure. Let me put some sneakers on. Are you ok?"

"Yea. I was just tired." I got my things and we left.

The entire ride over we listened to depressing ass love songs. I glanced at her and saw her wipe a few tears as she sung along with the song *Can't let go* by Mariah Carey. It was an old song but if you knew the words, you know she was singing about a breakup and how she couldn't let go but I was unaware about it.

"Hi. Just the two of you or will someone else be joining?" The waitress asked waiting for us to respond.

"No just the two of us." She smiled and ushered us to a booth.

"Where the fuck have you been Journey?" I heard my brother say as he stood over us. She ignored him and continued looking at the menu. He wasn't staring at her like he was about to attack.

"Venus, I want to try these lobster nachos. And I think these mussels too for the appetizer. What about you?? Colby chuckled, snatched the menu out her hand and yanked her out the booth. I stood up to try and intervene, but he was dragging her out the door. I told the waitress we would be right back but to bring out two sprites. I got outside and he had Journey hemmed the fuck up against the wall.

"I've been looking for you for four days Journey. Why haven't you been home or better yet why won't you take my calls?"

"I told you it was over Colby."

"And I fucking told you it wasn't."

"Wait a minute. Y'all broke up?" I asked both of them, but no one answered. Journey had tears coming down her face and Colby still had her against the wall.

"No we didn't break up. Journey is on some bullshit."

"Let me go Colby. I don't want to be with you anymore."

"Fuck that. You're not even telling me why. That dumb ass excuse you gave me didn't even make sense. Tell me what the fuck it is. Stop playing these childish ass games."

"What's going on? And Colby why do you have her against the wall like that?" I turned around and it was his ex-Willow. I turned back around, and Journey snatched away from him.

169

"Yea Colby tell her what's going on? Wait, are you two here together?" Journey asked and she had a smirk on her face.

"Yea. I went to the bathroom and came back only for the waitress to say he walked out with another woman. What's this about Colby?"

"You're questioning me nigga and you're out here on a date with your ex. You're a fucking joke. Venus can we go I lost my appetite?"

"Journey it's not what it looks like." He tried to say but Journey wasn't hearing anything, and I don't blame her.

"Don't believe him Journey. It's exactly what it looks like. Colby tell her how we just came from fucking at my house." The look on my brothers' face was nothing like I've ever seen. It was mixed with embarrassment and anger.

I grabbed Journey up and went back in the restaurant to get our things. We came back out and the two of them were standing there arguing.

"Journey wait!"

"Get the hell out of my face Colby." She turned around.

"I told you in the very beginning if you planned on

going back to her to leave my house before the morning and you told me it was nothing. You were supposed to protect my heart not break it. Stay the fuck away from me."

"I can't do that Journey." I turned around and he was pointing a gun at her.

"Oh my God Colby. What are you doing?" I yelled out standing in front of her. I knew he wouldn't shoot me, but I wasn't sure about Journey.

"I can't let you go Journey. I'm sorry."

"I told you he wasn't who you thought he was." Willow said making Colby look at her.

"When did you talk to her?" I heard Colby ask Willow.

"The other day when I saw her at the doctor's office. She knows everything Colby; including you telling me you still loved me."

"I don't love you. I told you that because you were sucking my dick and kept stopping when I was about to nut. You're a dumb bitch and did you record us?"

"Ugh yea. I knew she wouldn't believe me if I told her, so I needed proof." Colby shook his head and focused back on

Journey who had moved me out the way and stood in front of him.

"If you're going to kill me for falling in love with you and not tolerating you cheating and disrespecting me then do it. I'm not going to beg for my life because my parents didn't when they were in the same position I am right now." I turned around and saw the tears pouring down her face and that's when I knew she witnessed her parents being murdered.

Phew! Phew! I heard and Willow hit the ground.

"You talk too fucking much." Colby said looking down at Willow. He looked at Journey who was staring at him crying.

"I'm sorry Journey. I love the fuck out of you and it's so much shit I wanna say. I know you don't understand what's going on and neither do I but maybe you're right and we don't need to be together. Goodbye."

"Wait! What?" Journey yelled out and Colby walked away. I thought he was going to kill himself and I think she did too. I grabbed her hand and ran to the car because I could hear the cops coming. I wasn't sure who saw what, but we had to get the fuck out of there.

We got back to the house and both of us noticed Jax and Wolf were there. I assumed they were packing up the car to take some stuff to the other house but that wasn't the case. They were standing in the kitchen leaning against the counter with their arms folded. Those gray eyes they stared at us with looked scarier than ever.

"Somebody better tell me right fucking now why your brother Colby had a gun pointed at my sister. Before you ask it doesn't matter who told me." Wolf said in a tone that made the two of us think before we answered.

"Colby is the guy I've been seeing for the last few months."

"WHAT?" Wolf was pissed. Jax stood there shaking his head with a disappointing look. He was probably trying to figure out why I didn't tell him but it wasn't my business.

"Calm down Wolf. I don't need you going out there trying to retaliate."

"Don't tell me what the fuck to do Journey. You walk up in here with a fucking non chalant attitude about a nigga

173

pulling a gun out on you and you tell me to relax. Since when did you allow a man to treat you with that much disrespect? Huh?" Jax gave me a look not to get in the middle of it and as bad as I wanted to, I kept my mouth shut.

This was a side of Wolf I have never seen. His chest was poking out I guess from him being so angry, those fang teeth things he had were showing. I can see now why he got the name.

"Wolf stop treating me like I'm a fucking kid. He was mad because we broke up. Look, I'm not dead. Ok its over. He left, I left, and we can move on with our lives."

"Journey, I swear to God if you weren't my sister, I would put a fucking bullet in your head."

"Yo, Wolf you bugging now." Jax told him.

"You know what. Since everybody seems to be ok that some fuck nigga almost killed your sister." I noticed how he didn't say ours.

"Then you deal with it."

"Wolf come on. You know she isn't looking at it like that."

"Well guess what? I can't watch another one of my family members die and whether I was there or not when he did it, her dying would've been like watching it again. So excuse me for giving a fuck."

"Haven." Journey called him a name I never heard. He snapped his neck back and gave her an evil look.

"Don't say a fucking word to me. Don't call my phone, don't look for me on holidays, just don't say shit to me Journey." Her facial expression showed all the hurt he just instilled on her with those words.

"All our life I've kept you out of harm's way and if anybody, and I mean anybody even had a thought about bothering you they would end up dead. Now you're sitting in my face telling me not to get at him because you're not dead so it's ok." He chuckled.

"I know you're grown and can make your own decisions so that's what I'm going to let you do. If he does it again and kills you don't expect me at your funeral." He slammed the door and Jax ran behind him. Journey fell to the ground crying harder and I sat there comforting her. I didn't know what to do because the way Wolf acting towards her would be the same way my brothers would've acted if it were me.

Wolf

I had to leave Venus house before I put my hands on Journey and that was something I never wanted to do. My parents were probably cursing my sister out for allowing the nigga to get away with that shit. I could tell she loved him otherwise we would've met him.

Journey never wanted us to meet her friends unless she was really into him. She would tell us by then it wouldn't matter if we approved because they were already in love. Honestly, I've never met any guy she's been with so her hiding him didn't cross me as odd. What did peek my interest is the fact the nigga didn't even tell us he was fucking my sister? I felt my phone vibrating on my hip and picked it up only to see it was Jax calling me.

"What?"

"You good bro?" He asked.

"Never been better."

"Wolf, I know you're mad and I am too but the way you came off on Journey was kind of rough. Don't get me wrong though, her saying she not dead shit pissed me off too but you know she doesn't know how to deal with men like you and I. At the end of the day Colby is a savage just like us."

"Isn't it strange that he didn't tell us he was with her?" I didn't want to use fucking and Journey in the same sentence again. That's just weird to me.

"It is, but I'm not so sure he knows we're related. He knows I'm with his sister. I don't see him hiding him and Journey being a couple."

"If you say so."

"Where you on your way to?"

"I'm just driving right now. I'll hit you up later." I told him and pulled in the parking lot of the condo I had Passion staying in.

Lately she and I have been seeing a lot of each other. She would work and take her son to day care that I paid up to a year for. Then she would come home and cater to his every need. It's a shame men make these babies out here and then leave the women to fend for themselves. I have seen some men step up and take their kids too but nine times out of ten it's the other way around. I knocked on the door and waited for her to answer.

"I told you not to knock. You have the other key." She said walking away from the door. I could smell the food cooking and my stomach was growling. I walked in to see what she made, and it was steak, potatoes, green beans and it looked like macaroni and cheese.

"You must have a date making all this food."

"Please. I was hungry and you come over every night to check on us, so I decided to make you something to eat." I leaned on the counter with my arms folded and watched her put our food on a plate and take it to the table. Her son was coming around to me in his walker and put his hands up for me to pick him up. I was growing attached to him and I know I shouldn't have but it was hard when I was there almost everyday.

"Can you put him in the high chair so I could feed him mashed potatoes?" I did what she asked and sat at the table with them. This reminded me of my mom when she would make us have a family dinner every Sunday.

I watched her blow his food then feed him. Of course he would spit some out. I could see myself with a family but I'm not sure when.

After we ate, I helped her clean up then she gave lil man a bath. By the time he fell asleep it was after nine and I was tired myself. I heard the shower going and figured she was probably about to take it down to. I knocked on the door and told her I was staying over in the guest room like I did some nights because I didn't feel like driving home.

It was a three bedroom, so I wasn't taking up space from her and the baby. I took my clothes off and jumped in the shower. I thought about everything that happened today and still couldn't get the thought of Colby not mentioning him and my sister being a couple out of my head. I feel like something was up but I couldn't put my finger on it.

I turned the water off after I washed and grabbed a towel to walk in the room. I still had clothes and other things over here I moved into the guest room so she could have her own space. I put some pajama pants on, shut my door and I don't even remember when I fell asleep.

"What the fuck?" I jumped up out my sleep when I felt someone on top of me.

"You're going to shoot me." She asked because the gun was touching her forehead. I slept with it on the side of the bed. I put it on the nightstand and looked at her. She picked the remote up and shut the television off. I could see her silhouette and it was a sight to see.

"What you doing shorty?" I asked her.

"Wolf, I saw how upset you looked when you came in. I just want to make you feel better." She whispered in my ear and then started sucking on it.

"You don't have to." I could feel myself becoming aroused and wanted to stop her, but she wasn't trying to hear anything I was saying.

"I want to. I want you." I felt her kissing down my chest and on my stomach. I lifted up a little to help her get my pajama pants down. I free balled so there were no boxers.

"Damn, your dick big as hell." She said and we both started laughing.

"I told you we didn't have to." Was all I got out when

she started sucking? She made the slurping sounds and jerked me off at the same time. She put my hand on her head for me to guide her but I wrapped my hand around her hair and pulled her up.

"You sure you want this dick." I asked and turned my head when she tried to kiss me. She took both of her hands, held my face still and placed a soft kiss on my lips. She ran her tongue over my top lip and then the bottom without separating them. She did this a few times and the shit had me hard as ever. I just said fuck it and gave her my tongue since that's what she was hinting at.

"Mmmm. Wolf. I'm ready." She said when I stopped kissing her. I didn't say anything and flipped her on her back.

I kissed her again and caressed each of breast gently with my hand. I sucked on her neck and then found my way to her nipples that were already hard. I sucked on each one and made sure she got the same amount of pleasure with both of them. I let my hand slide up and down her slit and she was wet just like I knew she was. She took my hand and placed those fingers in her mouth and sucked all her juices off.

182

"Shit girl. That was for me."

"There's more where it came from." She said and put my hand back down there. Usually I don't give head but with her I wanted to. I attacked her entire pussy like I was in a pussy eating contest.

"Oh my God Wolf. I can't cum anymore. Baby please get up." She screamed out and tried to lift my head but this is what she wanted.

I gave her a few more orgasms, moved up to her lips and let both of us taste her. She wrapped her hands around my neck and her legs were around my waist. I pushed my man inside and almost drowned. She was so fucking wet that I had to pull out to keep from cumming. I've never had a girl get that wet but then again, I don't eat pussy like a lot either.

"Wolf, I'm cumming again. Oh shit. Oh shit. Fuckkkkk." I felt her release on me. I pushed her legs back and went deeper. I hit spots that had her trying to find a voice.

I made her get on top and she couldn't handle all of me. She stood on her feet and did a way better job that way. The shit was so good I had to make her jump off because it was my turn to cum. I didn't expect to fuck her and my condoms were

at my house. She came out the bathroom, washed us both up

and started jerking me off to get hard again.

"Word." I asked and she shook her head yes. I never

had a chick that could go more than one round so this was a

bonus for me. Once she got me hard, I made her get on all

fours and beat it up from the back. She was running but I kept

pulling her back.

"You said you wanted more. Don't run from it. If you

plan on fucking me, you have to get used to it." When I said

that it was like she turned into someone else. She started

throwing her ass back and I'll be damned if I didn't catch it.

"Just like that Passion. Damn that ass is jiggling nice.

Make it clap." When she did it, I came all inside her and

couldn't do shit about it. I fell back on the bed and she was

lying next to me.

"Wolf, I know you're not the guy to be in a relationship,

but I really like you and its not because you did all if this for

me but because you are a good person. I like the way you are

with my son, you respect me and haven't once tried to sleep

with me. I want you to be my man but before you say yes just know it means no other women and you have to be committed to me and only me." I chuckled at her ass.

"What are you laughing at?"

"I thought I was supposed to ask you to be my girl."

"You were taking too long."

"I was." She climbed back on top and got me hard. I didn't have a problem making her my girl if she was an all-nighter like this when it came to sex. I already knew she could cook, takes good care of her son and works her ass off even if it is at Wal-Mart.

"Shittttttttt Passion." I heard myself moan out when she slid down on my dick. It was harder for her to ride me if she was on her knees but on her feet it's the best rodeo I ever had.

"Are you going to be my man?"

"I don't know." I told her and she dropped down harder and my toes started curling.

"That's not the right answer."

"What's the right answer?" She did it again but this time she stayed down and grinded in circles on me. My eyes were rolling, and I felt myself about to nut.

"Yes, Passion yes. I'll be your man now make me cum hard." When I said that she turned around and rode me on her feet backwards. The sight of her ass jiggling when I smacked it and her moaning had me cum so hard, I had to make her sit there for a minute or two just to catch my breath.

"I love you Wolf." She said and passed the fuck out. Did she really love me? I mean women say the shit to me all the time after I fuck them. I guess only time will tell.

****

The next morning, she woke me up by giving me some more head and pussy, I'm assuming before the baby woke up. I guess this relationship won't be so bad after all if this is what I get to wake up to.

I looked at the clock and it was after ten. I went in the bathroom to get myself ready for the day. I came out and she was dressed in a pair of fitted jeans, a sweater and some timbs. Her hair was up in a ponytail and she never wore makeup.

"What's up?" I asked her putting on some jeans I kept over there.

186

"I don't have to work today but Venus has an opening to get my hair done. Can you drop me off?"

"Do you have your license?"

"Ugh yea. But I'm not driving that death trap you have out there." I laughed because I had the Maserati and not my truck with me. She said the car was too small the time I took her to work in it. It felt like a box and if anyone hit us we would be dead on impact.

"You weren't driving my car anyway." She stepped in my personal space.

"I already drove your car a few times last night."

"Yup and your ass was having problems too."

"You're right. That was until I stood up and rode the shit out of you." She went to walk away but I pulled her back.

"And I appreciate the fuck out of you for it." She stood on her tippy toes and kissed me. I backed her against the wall, ripped her sweater off and pulled her jeans and boots off. All she had on was a thong and bra. My dick was trying to break free.

"Turn the fuck around." She did like I said, and I separated her legs. I unsnapped the bra she wore, and she quickly removed the thongs. I let my jeans fall to my ankles and rammed my dick inside her without even making sure she was wet.

"Ahhh Wolf." She cried out.

"If you want Wolf to be your man then this pussy has to be ready on demand. You got that." She didn't answer and I figured it was because her cum was creaming all over my dick.

"Spread those legs wider." She did as I said, and I pulled her away from the wall just a little so she could arch her back. I fucked her harder and harder and she took ever pump like a champ. I bit down on her shoulder and had my fingers massaging her clit at the same time. Her body started jerking and shaking.

"Make it rain on my dick Passion." She wasn't cumming fast enough for me.

"NOW DAMMIT." I smacked her ass and not even two seconds later she came and almost fell because her legs gave out on her.

"Nah, we not done." I turned her around and lifted her up so she could slide down on me.

"Wolf. I can't take anymore."

"You wanted this Wolf dick? This is your dick, right?"

"Yes baby but..."

"But nothing. Fuck me back Passion." She started going up and down screaming out my name. She bit down on my neck.

"I'm cumming Passion. You know how to make your dick cum now do it." She squeezed her pussy muscles together as she went up and down. A few seconds later I let go inside of her again.

At this point she was my girl now so whatever happens, happens. I didn't want any kids right now, but I should've been more responsible. We both fell on the bed. I pulled her close to me and covered us both up. Neither one of us left the house.

****

My phone was ringing back to back and the shit was getting on my nerves. I had Passion lying on my chest and I was still trying to get a few hours of sleep in before I left. I

189

answered the phone without looking and it was Journey saying she was outside. I hung the phone up on her but Passion jumped up and threw some clothes on.

"What are you doing? I thought you were sleep."

"Babe, your phone woke me up too and you can't leave your sister outside."

"Fuck her." She stopped moving and looked at me.

"Don't say that. I like your sister and I don't know what's going on between y'all, but you need to fix it. You're never supposed to spend more than an hour mad at someone."

"I don't wanna talk to her."

"Awww baby. I promise if you talk to her, we can have that animal sex again like we had this morning."

"You liked that." I asked smiling.

"At first, I thought I wouldn't, but I don't think I've had sex better than that. The shit was so good I was dreaming about it."

"You silly as hell girl. Move." I told her and got up.

"I'm serious Wolf. And the growling you did when you came made it all worth it."

190

"Look what you did." I pointed to my dick that was now hard listening to her talk.

"Well you're going to have to wait because I just text your sister I was coming to open the door." She said with the phone in her hand. She is a trip but I can see us being together for a while.

Journey

I felt bad about what happened with Wolf and Colby. I don't know what was going on with either of them, but I was going to start with my brother first. He was hurt by what I said and when I went home and thought about it, he had every right to be. A man pulled a gun out on his sister and I brushed it off. He saw the same shit happen with my parents, so I know it was a lot going through his head.

I was upset he hung the phone up when I called but happy Passion sent me a text saying she was opening the door. I sat in my car waiting to get out because I wasn't sure if I should go in. I heard a knock on the window, and it was Wolf. I rolled it down to talk.

"What's up Journey?" He asked standing outside my truck.

"I'm sorry Wolf. I should've thought about what I said before I said it. I love you and Jax and I know you don't want anything to happen to me but some things I have to figure out on my own." He nodded his head and got inside on the passenger side.

"So did you figure out why he pulled a gun out on you?"

"No. Wolf, I wanted to tell you guys about him, but I didn't want you run him away."

"Do you love him?"

"Yes. I'm in love with him."

"Then why did you break up with him?"

"Because he cheated on me." I felt the tears coming down my face and tried to wipe them away. He pulled me close and laid my head on his shoulder.

"Did you ask him why?"

"No."

"Journey, you have the right to know why."

"I don't think I want to know."

"Why not?"

"I don't understand why he's the one who cheated, yet he won't allow me to break up with him. Wolf, I didn't know he was at the restaurant. He took me outside and asked me why

193

did I leave him and I couldn't tell him because I didn't want him to know is ex told me. I should've told him when she came to me, but I didn't. Then she came out and started talking shit and told on herself. When he found out it was her that told me he shot her twice." He lifted my head up.

"He shot her."

"Yea. He had the gun on me but Venus jumped in front of me. He wasn't going to shoot his sister and honestly, I don't think he would shoot me. If he wanted to, he wouldn't have hesitated. He damn sure didn't hesitate to shoot her. I don't even feel sorry for her."

"I can't get over the fact that you're ok with him doing that."

"I'm not Wolf but when I broke up with him, he told me things were complicated and he couldn't tell me what they were. Then after he shot her, he mentioned something else that stuck out to me."

"What?"

"There was so much shit he needed to tell me and its shit he doesn't even understand. Something is going on but I

194

can't figure out what it is. Venus doesn't know either, but she said he's never acted this way over anyone else."

"Is the ex named Willow?"

"Yes. How do you know who she is?"

"I used to fuck her and I'm the one who killed her sister." I covered my mouth.

"Do you think she has anything to do with what happened?" He asked me.

"She had everything to do with it. She hated me the first time she laid eyes on me and the day I found out I was pregnant, she couldn't wait to run out behind me and tell me she was sleeping with him."

"Hold up. You're pregnant?" I nodded my head and he put his head back on the seat and blew his breath out.

"That's why he didn't shoot you."

"He doesn't know."

"Journey you have to tell the man you're pregnant."

"I don't want to. Then he's really not going to leave me alone."

"Journey I'm not going to tell you what to do and you not being with him is one thing but not telling him about his kid is foul. Would you want me to treat a woman like that?"

"No. I guess not. And speaking of women, how's it going with Passion?" I changed the subject so I could stop crying.

"She asked me to be her man last night and I told her yea."

"She asked you. Fool it's supposed to be the other way around." I pushed him in the shoulder.

"I didn't know she was even interested."

"Boy please. Venus and I knew she wanted you the third day she was here." He shook his head laughing.

"Anyway, I was thinking about getting her a whip. I have to take her everywhere and I hate making her use the Uber service. What you think?"

"I think if she's your girl you're supposed to spoil her. But make sure she's ok with it. She's been through a lot with her son's father. She may not be willing to accept gifts."

"What chicks you know don't want a car?"

"Just take her to the dealership and peep her reaction when you tell her to pick a car. If she gets real excited then you know she'll most likely be ok with it. If she's skeptical then you have to take your time giving her things. She will have to get used to you supporting her since she's on her independent shit. And talk to her and tell her that whatever you get her you won't take back. Remember the punk took everything away from her." He nodded his head like he understood.

"Your boy gets one free pass. I swear Journey if he ever does that fuck shit again, you'll just have to be mad."

"Agreed. I love you Wolf."

"I love you too. Now let me go take this chick to get a car." He kissed my cheek and got out.

I drove to my house still in deep thought about what Colby meant by not understanding what was going on. I called Venus to see what she was up too, but my call went to voicemail and it was probably because she was at work. I contemplated on going home then I said fuck it and went to in the other direction.

When I pulled up to the house, I was nervous, scared and just feeling downright stupid but I had to know what was going on. I knocked on the door like a dummy. He always told me he couldn't hear and told people to ring the doorbell instead.

"Yes. How can I help you?" Some woman answered the door. She didn't look too old, but she wasn't young either. I guess he wanted a cougar now.

"Uhmmm. I was looking for Colby, but I can come back another time."

"Are you Journey?" The woman asked shocking the hell out of me.

"Yes. And you are?"

"I'm his aunt. Come in." She stepped aside and allowed me to walk in. I've been to this house a bunch of times but today it felt like the first. I heard some voices from the other room and they didn't sound like him.

"You are as beautiful as he said you were." I put my head down smiling. I always blushed when someone gave me a compliment.

"Who's at the door?" I heard a male voice say. I looked and it was a guy that resembled Colby, but it wasn't him.

"Yo, Colby I think you should come see who's at the door."

"I'm Wesley, Colby's brother." He extended his hand.

"Hi, I'm..."

"Journey. I know who you are." How the hell did everyone know who I was, but I had no clue who they were?

"Who is it?" Colby said. He stopped when he saw me.

It was like time stood still as we stared at each other. Neither of us spoke and I could hear voices around me but I couldn't tell you what was being said. After a few minutes of standing there he finally spoke.

"What are you doing here Journey?"

"I came to see you."

"Journey, I did some fuck shit and pulled a gun out on you. Why would you want to see me after that?"

"Because it wasn't you Colby." I moved in closer to him and ran my hand down his face. He put his hand on top of mine and kissed it.

199

"I don't know what's going on but I want you to tell me. I also want to know why you cheated on me?"

"Journey, I can't say it without hurting you and I've done enough of that. Just know that I didn't know I would fall in love with you. If I did, I never would've agreed to anything."

"Colby you're confusing me. What did you agree to?"

"Just go Journey. We're not together anymore so I don't owe you an explanation. Just go and forget about me, us and whatever we had."

"I CAN'T COLBY. DON'T YOU THINK IF I COULD, I WOULD?" I found myself yelling and crying again. He lifted my chin, kissed my lips and disappeared in the house somewhere. I was left standing there by myself while everyone stared at me. They must've come out when I was yelling.

"Just give him some time Journey. Whatever happened between the two of you has him going through some things of his own." His aunt said rubbing my back. I noticed Wesley following me out to my car. I opened the door and he stopped me.

"Does he know about the baby?"

"Excuse me."

"Does he know about the baby?"

"I don't know what you're talking about." He gave me the side eye.

"Journey the first day I saw you at the party you were very petite. Now your nose is a little bigger, you definitely look thicker and he may not have noticed but I see the little pouch in your stomach." I broke down crying again. He gave me a hug until I stopped.

"Journey my brother loves you and the things you think you want to know, you don't. Nothing he did was because he wanted to, it was more like he was forced."

"He was forced to cheat on me?"

"Yes and no."

"Huh?"

"Yes, he was forced, blackmailed or whatever you want to call it to cheat on you. He had a choice with that person who knew what he was told to do. She told him if he didn't sleep with her, she would tell you and that alone made him sick. He hated that he didn't make the right choice and cheated but he also didn't want you to leave him when you found out. So he did what he thought was right and tried to keep both things hidden but as you can see it didn't work out in his favor."

"But why won't he talk to me? He could've just told me what it was and let me make the choice to stay with him."

"I don't think you understand my brother. He's not your typical man that's ok with hurting woman. Believe it or not he never cheated on his ex but because she thought he did, she did. When you came in his life there was a reason and at first, he didn't give a fuck about hurting you but then you got in his heart somehow and he couldn't fathom anyone causing you harm, himself included. Him and my father are at war right now over you. The two of you may not be together but just know he's making sure no one bothers you."

"I'm trying to see it from your point of view, but I can't unless I know everything that's going on."

"I understand but to be honest we don't even know what's going on. I'm going to talk to him and try to get him to tell you but you have to give him a chance to tell you without flying off the deep end."

"Ok. Should I wait here?"

"No. Go home and wait for him there. I promise you he'll be over tonight even if I have to bring him there myself." I gave him a hug and got in my car to go home. I was anxious, nervous and scared to see him but I wanted to know what was going on.

Once I got home, I showered and laid in my bed. All I could do now was wait and hope he came to tell me what was going on.

Wolf

After Journey left the house, I went back upstairs and Passion was just getting out the shower. I saw the hickeys I left on her and smiled. It was weird having a chick but I was going to try and be on my best behavior. The way we've fucked over the last three days I know for damn sure I didn't want anyone else to have her.

Once I finished getting myself together, I looked at the clock and it was a little after two in the afternoon. I still had time to get her a new car and pick the baby up from day care. I told her to have Venus set her up with an appointment for tomorrow since she missed todays.

I took Passion to the car dealership and Journey was right about paying attention to her reaction when I told her to pick out a car. She was very hesitant and asked if the car was going to be in her name. She picked out a midnight blue 2016 BMW X6. It was fully loaded with the backup camera, Sirius radio and all the new shit that came along with it.

I had them put all her information on the truck and told them to give her temporary insurance. When we got home, she could go online and find one at a cheaper rate.

"Thank you Haven."

"Yo. Don't call me that." I hated she knew my real name.

"Why? I like it."

"Yea, well only my sister and Grams call me that. If you stick around long enough maybe, I'll be ok with you using it."

"With the thing you got in between your legs and that tongue, I'm not going anywhere." She said.

"Oh yea."

"Hell yea. After the baby goes to sleep, I want some more."

"I don't know about all that. I may have to put you on a schedule." I told her and she frowned her face up.

"Yea right. Are you coming over tonight?" She asked getting in her car.

"Do you want me to?"

"You're my man now. You better."

"Whatever. I'm going back to the house. After you pick lil man up come get me so we could go out to eat." I put my head in her window, she slipped her tongue in my mouth and kissed me like we were home.

"You play too much. Look what you did." I said pointing to my dick that was hard.

"That's what you get."

"Maybe I should go find someone to handle it then."

"Don't play with me Wolf? You see this pretty face, but I will hurt you and that bitch."

"Take your ass to pick lil man up and I'll see you when you get back." She pulled off and I got back in my car to head to the condo. I parked in the spot and went inside and found myself lying down. I must've dosed off because Passion came in kissing me.

"You ready babe?" She was holding the baby waiting for me to get up.

"Yea, let me brush my teeth and we can go."

When I was done, we hopped in her new ride and ended up at The Outback Steakhouse for dinner. The place wasn't too crowded and we were seated pretty quick. The waitress came over and took our order but not without throwing shade at Passion who in return was ready to fight.

Yea, I slept with the waitress once and didn't call her after but that was because her pussy was garbage. The manager came over and told us the food was on the house. It was the summer and it didn't get dark until nine and it was only seven. We left and stopped by a park for a little while. We were getting ready to leave when two black suburban's blocked us in. Passion started panicking right away.

"Calm down Passion. I'm not going to allow anything to happen to you."

"But it's so many of them." I looked out the window and four people got out of one and no one came out of the other. I sent a message to Drew and told him to get here quick.

"Passion, you said you loved me right?" She nodded her head yes.

"Did you mean it?"

207

"I do."

"Ok then I'm not going to let someone who loves me get hurt. You should know me better than that." She nodded her head.

"Wipe your tears and try and sit here without looking upset. I don't want them to think you're weak because they'll play on it."

"Ok. How do I look?" She said after wiping her tears and started looking in the mirror.

"You're fine. Remind me to take you to the shooting range."

"Be careful." She said and turned me around to kiss her before I got out the car. Most people will wonder why I got out but what was I going to sit inside for? If they wanted to shoot me it would've already happened.

I opened the door and stood up stretching. I wasn't going to give them any inclination I was nervous or trying to run. I closed the door and walked over to the suburban behind the truck. The window came down and the same older guy who was at the chick's funeral was staring at me.

"Listen, before this goes any further, I want you to allow her to leave." He laughed like the shit was funny and so did the guys standing there from the other truck. I pulled a blunt from behind my ear and lit it. They all watched me without saying a word.

Phew! Phew! Phew! Phew!

"Damn my aim is still perfect." I said after laying all four of those men out in less than ten seconds. The man nodded his head and the suburban moved back. I walked over to the driver's side and told Passion to roll her window down.

"Park down the street and wait for me. If I'm not back in the car in ten minutes pull off and call my sister. Do not and I repeat, do not go back to the condo because I'm sure they'll come there for you. Pull the car in the back yard at your sister's house and stay there until you here from me or my brother. Don't answer any unknown calls?"

"I don't know your brothers' number."

"He will send you a text first. Now do what I said and start the clock when you park. That will give me time to see what this motherfucker wants." She nodded her head and asked

209

me for another kiss. I hate that I had to tell her no but I didn't want them to assume we were a couple. Enemies always go after the girlfriend. They can assume all they want but until its verified I won't give them any hints.

I waited until I saw she was out of sight and went to the other suburban. Whoever this dude was already had people out here cleaning up his mess. I stood against the tree waiting for him to come to me. Shit, if he followed me then it was for a reason. He finally stepped out and I give it to him, he was dressed to impress with his Armani suit and gator shoes. He was smoking a cigar and talking on the phone to someone.

"Hello Haven or should I call you Wolf?"

"Don't call me shit. Just tell me what you want." He chuckled and flicked his ashes on the ground.

"I wanted your sister, but it seems like the plan I had to get her failed when my dumb ass son fell in love with her."

"What the fuck did you just say?"

"Oh, that's right you didn't know. My son is Colby and I hired him to kill your sister." I was so fucking mad because I knew the nigga was up to something. I punched the old man in

210

his face and felt two people grab me from behind. He ran his hand over his jaw and spit out a little blood on my shoe.

"If anything happens to my sister, I swear to God you'll be burying that nigga Colby."

"Oh, like I had to bury my son Dice." When he said that, I stopped and looked at him. Once I took a good look, I saw the resemblance between him and Colby and him and Venus. I don't remember Dice as much because it happened so long ago.

"Just like I had to bury not one but both of my parents because your son was a greedy fuck."

"No, your father owed me money."

"And he paid it. Your son was there trying to collect extra."

"He never told me that."

"I bet he didn't. You raised a greedy motherfucker that killed my parents' and planned on killing me and my siblings had I not got to him first." I could see him thinking about what I said.

"When he told me he killed your parents I did feel bad. Your father and I never had beef. I was willing to compensate for your loss, but you took my son."

"Compensate motherfucker?" You can't compensate my parents. This isn't some sort of slip and fall. He killed them and laughed after he did it."

"Well that's too bad. Do you know how hard it was laying my son to rest? His mother was dying from cancer and his other siblings cried every night."

"Like I give a fuck. My mother and father were shot in front of me. At least you didn't see him suffer and get stepped on like he was nothing. My house was destroyed, and your son had people looking for me. I don't feel bad for you one bit. But like I said." I stood toe to toe with him.

"If my sister has one piece of hair touched, I will touch that nigga Colby, your daughter Venus, the other son you think I don't know about and I will come for you last."

"Your threats don't scare me son."

"They shouldn't. Just like yours don't." I felt a sharp pain in the back on my leg and another one on my side. I grabbed my gun and started shooting back, to who I have no idea.

I saw Drew running up and more black trucks started pulling in the park. It was so many people jumping out shooting I don't know who was who. I saw that old nigga jump in his truck and let as many shots off as I could.

I made it to Passion's car and was happy as hell she didn't pull off even though it had been more than ten minutes.

"Get me to the hospital." She put her foot on the gas and started speeding. I told her to hand me her phone. I dialed my sisters' number and was hoping she answered.

"Make sure Journey is ok." Was the last thing I said before everything went black?

Colby

I looked out the window and saw Wesley hugging Journey as she cried. It was killing me to know I was the reason behind it. Instead of hurting her anymore it was best for us to be apart even if it's not what I wanted. My brother cursed my ass out when I told him what I did while my father asked why I didn't kill her. I tried to strangle his ass when he said that shit. Wesley and one of the guards had to pull me away from him.

My father was going through a lot to get at Journey and I don't know why. What I did know is, I had someone watching her at all times. Yea, they told me she was hugged up with the nigga Wolf but it's temporary. Journey was mine and no one was taking her away from me.

I walked downstairs and everyone was staring at me. My aunt rolled her eyes and walked out the room. My cousins who were visiting were teenagers and did the same thing. I guess it was a woman thing because my uncle stayed there watching television.

I sat next to him and took my phone out to see if I had any messages. I heard Willow didn't die and was going home in a few days and that was fine because I didn't try to kill her. I wanted her to know the blackmailing me shit was over and me shooting her was just a warning. My boy delivered a message for me at the hospital and I haven't heard a peep from her. The cops couldn't identify me because the outside cameras were broken, and I was happy about that.

"Yo! Colby come here real quick." Wesley called out when he came in.

"What's up?"

"You know I don't usually get in your business, but you need to talk to her."

"Nah, I'm good. She'll be fine in a few days."

"I told her you'll be over there tonight. I suggest you put your big boy pants on and just tell her everything. If you feel like you lost her it won't matter what you say but she has the right to know Colby. You can't leave her out there in the blind."

I walked away and went upstairs in my room to decide what I wanted to do. I guess now that me sleeping with my ex is out in the open what more do I have to lose. I jumped in the shower, threw some sweats on and drove to her house. I didn't see her grandmothers' car, so I assumed she was home alone.

I rang the doorbell once and no one answered. I rang it the second time and she opened it. I noticed something was different about her. She stepped aside to let me in and closed the door behind me. I followed her up to her room and sat on the edge of the bed while she went to get under the covers.

"Why did you cheat on me?"

"I didn't want to Journey. Please believe me when I say that."

"Then why did you?" I moved closer to her.

"The day I met you wasn't by accident." She looked confused.

"I work for my father and he pays me to kill people." She covered her mouth, but I moved her hands.

"I'm not going to kill you. Well not now anyway."

"You were going to kill me."

216

"Yes."

"But why?"

"My father called me in his office and handed me a file with all of your

information in it. Fortunately, for me you were going to the same college I was so it would be easier to get to you. I knew everything about you as far as where you lived, worked, interned at, shopped and anything else. I was unaware you had brothers or that your parents were killed. None of it was in the information he gave me.

However, the day I met you and you basically flipped me off I was intrigued. Then you came to my house and had my full attention. You were smart, gorgeous and had a good head on your shoulders. You had a clean record and you weren't a ratchet chick. I couldn't understand why he wanted you dead."

"Wait. So you knew all this and were still going to do it?"

"Unfortunately, I was." I saw her pull her knees to her chest like she was scared.

217

"Journey it was before I fell in love with you, which happened quick. Whenever I was around you, you made me want to change my life around. I no longer wanted to kill and wanted to have a family with you."

"You should've told me."

"I tried."

"When?" She questioned.

"The first night I made love to you I tried but you wouldn't let me talk. You assumed I was going to say something about my ex but I wasn't. I found enough courage to tell you but you shut me down and as time went on I said fuck it."

"Colby."

"Let me finish. The day I made it official with you I went by her house because as you know she was blowing my phone up. I told her it was over. I even had my hand on the door to leave but she threatened to tell you and I couldn't fathom the thought of you hurting. In the end, I messed around and hurt you anyway." I wiped her tears.

"You just don't know how much it's killing me that we can't be together." I pecked her lips.

"Baby, I love you so much but right now me being here is dangerous. If anyone hurts you because of me I will never forgive myself."

"Why does your father want me dead?"

"To this day he will not answer that question for me when I ask. And trust me I've asked a thousand times."

"What's crazy is I don't even know him and have no idea why anyone would want me dead." I agreed.

"I miss you Journey and I'm sorry I brought this hurt and pain into your life. You are a good woman and didn't deserve it." She sat there crying and my heart was aching for her but what could I do? There was no way we could be together without one of us getting killed.

"Why did you do this to us? I love you so much Colby and I can't be without you. I need you."

"Baby don't cry." I sat behind her and she laid her head back on my chest. She moved my hand to her stomach and left it there. I moved her forward and had her face me.

"Are you pregnant?" I asked. She shook her head yes and my smile made her smile.

"How many months are you?" I rubbed her stomach with a big grin on my face.

"Three months. I got pregnant when you broke my virginity."

"Move in with me."

"Colby you just said we can't be together and it's dangerous."

"I know but scratch that. I can't protect you and my baby over here."

"I'm not sure about coming to your house but I'll stay over when you want me to."

"It's not the same babe but I understand. Just know I'm going to be here everyday and night so I'm going to need a key. I'm not missing any moments with our baby."

"Are you really happy?"

"Hell yea I'm happy. I can't wait to see my son playing football."

"What if it's a girl?"

"I guess I can take her to cheerleading practice." She and I sat up talking for a while.

"Now what?"

"Now that you know everything, I want you in my life Journey. I don't want to go another day without knowing you're my girl."

"I have to think about it."

"And I'll be here every day until you do." I stood up, took my clothes off and got in the bed with her. As much as I wanted to make love to her I wouldn't. I wanted her to make the first move.

"I love you Colby."

"I love you too Journey."

****

"Wake y'all asses up. Got some nigga downstairs banging on my door looking for you at eight in the damn morning." She looked at me and I shrugged my shoulders.

"I'm not talking about him girl. I'm talking about your ass." It was time for her to shrug my shoulders. She stood up, went in the bathroom to brush her teeth and wash her face. I

221

came in behind her and grabbed my toothbrush and did the same.

"Put some clothes on." I said with a mouth full of toothpaste.

"I have clothes on."

"Don't play with me." I said and she looked down. She had on some boy shorts and white wife beater. She put some leggings on and a t-shirt before she went down there. She left the door open and as I walked out, I could hear her talking.

"Hey sexy. Long time no see." The guy said, reaching for a hug but she pushed him back.

"What do you want Maurice?"

"I came to tell you, I miss you and want you back."

"Too bad nigga, she's taken. Get your goofy ass the fuck up out of here."

"Who is this Journey and why is he coming from upstairs."

"You're a dumb motherfucker. If I said she's taken it's obvious I'm her man. I'm coming from her room because that's what we do."

"I know you didn't give this thug your virginity and not me."

Phew! Phew! I shot his ass in the head twice. Who the fuck did he think he was questioning my woman? He should've left when he had the chance. I sent a text to Wesley and told him to send someone over to clean up the mess I made.

"Umm, uhmmm, uhmmm. Girl you got this nigga killing over you. You better not ever leave his crazy ass. I may not find you." Her grandmother said laughing and walked away. She didn't even care a man was dead in the house.

"Colby, I know I never told you about my parents but if I plan on being with you, I'm going to tell you and I don't want you to do that in front of me again." I nodded my head. We sat in the kitchen while she made us something to eat.

"One night my mom could be heard downstairs begging my dad to pay someone money. My father paid the money but whoever the guy was tacked on four thousand dollars for interest."

"Damn that's a lot."

"That's the same thing my dad said. He didn't pay it and said he wasn't. That night he called my brother Haven in the room and gave him money to buy us cell phones, summer clothes and to put the rest away. Two weeks went by and it seemed like everything was fine. The night my parents were killed was like any other night. We had just finished eating dinner, had taken our showers and were getting ready for bed. We heard yelling downstairs and Haven told us to come in his room.

There was a secret door in his closet that had just enough room to fit the three of us in it just in case something happened. Haven made me and my brother get in and went back out to see what was going on. He didn't know, but I came out to look also." mI could hear her getting choked up.

"I watched as this man came in and took both of my parents' life like they were nothing. Neither of my parents begged for their lives. After he killed them, he stepped on my father's back like he was a piece of the floor.

I ran back in the closet and a few minutes later Haven was coming in behind me. We heard the men yelling out for us

224

but none of us moved. We stayed quiet and fell asleep in there. When we came out the next morning our house was trashed, and my parents' bodies were gone. It wasn't until two days later when the cops found them miles away from here and broadcasted it on the news." I saw her crying and the eggs were burning. I ran up behind her, cut the stove off and hugged her. Now I see why she said that when I pulled a gun out on her. I see why she didn't like violence. To see your own parents murdered in cold blood was nothing I would wish on anyone.

"Did they catch the guys who did it?"

"No. I'm sure he's still out there somewhere."

"Do you know his name?"

"I will never forget his name or face. It's embedded in my head forever. Colby I'm not a killer but if I ever saw him again, I would take his life the way he took my mom and dads."

"What was his name?"

"Dice." It felt like the wind was knocked out of me when she said it. I let her go and fell back against the wall.

There was no way this could be happening right now. But it all started coming together. The reason why I was sent to do this. I had to get outta this house.

"Colby are you ok?" She asked wiping her face, but I couldn't answer her. My words were caught in my throat. I know Dice is the right person she named because no one else had that name around here. I ran up to her room, grabbed my keys, and sprinted to my car. I passed the guys cleaning the mess up and called Wesley.

"Yo, meet me at pops NOW!" I said in the phone and hung up. I was racing down the highway trying to get there. When I got there, he was standing outside talking to the gardener.

"You motherfucker. You knew, didn't you? You fucking knew." He started laughing. I punched him in the face and kept punching him until I felt people pulling me off him.

"What's going on?" Wesley said holding me against my car.

"This motherfucker is the reason Dice is dead."

"Dice. Why are you bringing him up?"

226

"Don't you want to know why our brother was killed?" When I said that Wesley let go and turned around and gave my father the evilest look.

"Who killed him?"

"I don't know that yet. I know he sent Dice to kill Journey's parents, and whoever killed Dice must've found out he did it and went after him. Your father sent me to Journey to find out from her who did it and then kill her. You had me do all that and she doesn't even know."

"No but I do and you taking her out would've given me the satisfaction of watching that motherfucker suffer. His entire life is based around Journey and he will go crazy if anything happened to her. You're lucky she was able to tame the beast because he was coming for you after you pulled a gun on her." He was getting up off the ground and spitting out blood.

"Who the fuck you talking about?" I asked.

"Don't worry. You'll know in due time." He laughed.

"I may have missed him the night at the club but I won't miss again."

"I thought you were worried about Venus that night. Did you set the shit up knowing she was in there?" Wesley asked now pissed.

"I didn't know she would be there but it was my doing. He killed that stupid bitch and a few of my good men. It's only a matter of time before he gets what's coming to him. Matter of fact, if I were you, I would find my way back to the girl. It would be a shame if something were to happen to her because you left her unattended." When he said that, I was a nervous fucking wreck.

I jumped back in my car and flew back to her house. When I got there the cops and ambulance was covering the driveway and putting up caution tape.

"Baby, what happened?" I asked when I bombarded my way in the house and saw her standing there with her grandmother.

"I don't know Colby. After you left, Grams and I were sitting in the kitchen talking when she said she saw someone in the back yard. She made me hide in her room and when she yelled for me to come out there were two dead bodies in the kitchen. She said they came in and she hid in the kitchen closet.

"Your grandmother has a gun?"

"Hell yea I got a gun. It's registered too. I know who your father is and I've never trusted him. I told my son he was a grimy motherfucker and that he was going to get him killed."

Now I was confused as hell.

"Hold on." Journey said and answered her phone.

"Hey Passion. What? Oh my God. I'll be there in a few minutes."

"What's the matter?"

"Grams, Haven got shot and he's at the hospital."

"I'll drive you." I told her and the three of us jumped in the car.

"Jax, where are you? Haven got shot. Ok, I'll meet you at the hospital." She yelled in the phone.

"Oh my God, please let him make it. I can't take it if he dies."

"He's going to be fine Journey. Try and relax. You can't stress the baby out." I told her.

229

"Oh so you know?" Her grandmother asked.

"Yup and I'm happy as hell."

"Are y'all back together?"

"It's up to her. I was the one who lied and cheated trying to hide something from her when I should've just been up front. I love Journey and I understand she needs time to make her decision. But you can bet I'll be here everyday until she makes one. And if she comes back with a no, I'll still be here until she changes her mind."

"Make him suffer baby."

"Of course grandma. You didn't raise no fool."

"That's cold Grams. I thought you loved me."

"I do. But I love Journey more and you have to suffer enough so it won't happen again."

"Trust me, it won't." We pulled up at the emergency room and she ran over to some chick that I guess was his Haven's girlfriend. I saw Jax walk in with my sister and was a bit confused. I know she called him, but I thought it was for Venus to comfort her. Those two exchanged hugs and I wasn't too happy about that.

"What are you doing here?" Venus asked and pulled me to the side.

"What you mean? I brought Grams and Journey. She said her brother was shot." As I was telling her, Wesley walked in mad as hell and came straight to Venus and I.

"Where is that motherfucker?" He yelled out which made everyone look; including Jax.

"Who?" I had no idea who he was speaking of.

"The motherfucker that killed Dice."

"Dice? How do you know him?" Journey came to where we were. The three of us stood there not saying a word.

"Colby tell me you didn't know the man that killed my parents." Venus covered her mouth and started crying and Wesley had a sympathetic look. I was just staring at her because I forgot to tell her when I got back to the house.

"The family of Haven Banks." The doctor came out to say something, but all that shit was cut short when I heard the gun cock.

"If you came here to kill my brother, then I suggest you ask God to forgive you for your sins because I'm about to blow your fucking head off."

TO BE CONTINUED....